A MILLION TO ONE

A Novel

A MILLION TO ONE

Ed deMartin

iUniverse, Inc.
New York   Bloomington

A Million To One

iUniverse books may be ordered through booksellers or by contacting:

iUniverse
1663 Liberty Drive
Bloomington, IN 47403
www.iuniverse.com
1-800-Authors (1-800-288-4677)

ISBN: 978-1-4502-5826-5 (sc)
ISBN: 978-1-4502-6291-0 (dj)
ISBN: 978-1-4502-5827-2 (ebk)

Printed in the United States of America

iUniverse rev. date: 11/18/2010

This book is for Marie Dornwell deMartin
who gave me a second wonderful life.

And for Virginia Carroll deMartin
who gave me the first wonderful life, along with
Jon, Cathy, Michael and Missy.

Acknowledgements

To my muse Marie,
whose authentic riches to rags life
inspired a fictional story.
And who motivated and tolerated me
throughout its writing.

To Greg Dinallo, friend and successful novelist,
for guidance and encouragement to a rookie.

To AnnMarie and Frank LaForge, who read it
as I wrote it and kept asking for more.

To attorney Keith Harriton for his advice on
"The Celebrity Trial of the Decade", found herein.

To Michael DeMartin, the master of Designsite
and the world of cyber, for his invaluable assistance.

CHAPTER 1

Christmas, 1980 is just two weeks away. Sparkling lights, festive decorations and familiar carols can be seen and heard all over town. December 25th also happens to be Cassie Jean Dornwell's 21st birthday. She should be elated, but is not at all thrilled. Too many bad memories are tied to Noels and birthdays past.

According to every Christmas movie she's ever seen, it should be cold and snowing. But in Orlando, Florida it's eighty degrees and the Hibiscus are blooming. At 2:30 a.m., Cassie parks a twelve year old VW Beetle in front of the garage she calls home. Last night was long and hard. Like her used and abused car, she's running almost on empty.

Still dressed in the scanty outfit and silver stilettos worn at work, she climbs awkwardly out of the small auto. In the process, her skirt hikes up to the waist, revealing killer legs. The pretty young blonde is carrying two armfuls of Winn Dixie groceries. Closing the car door with her hip, she now girds herself for the struggle upstairs.

Heavy bags and six inch heels do not help matters as she climbs an outside flight of steep, narrow steps. On the way up, she asks herself, *Who needs gym workouts when you live over a garage?*

Breathing hard as she reaches her second-story destination, she sets the packages down on the top step. Fumbles through her shoulder bag for the right key. Finally swings the door open into a tiny efficiency kitchen. Where her brown kraft cargo drops on the counter with a dull thud.

Cassie and her six year old son Preston Jon, known to all as PJ, reside in this modest three room garage apartment, situated in a borderline lower class section of town. A neighborhood of small lots that push little houses together. One or two bedrooms, cinder block and stucco. Painted in pale, peeling colors. Yellows, pinks, peaches... here and there a chartreuse or a bright turquoise. Mostly retired people. Or young starter families. It's a seedy area with weedy lawns, but the racially mixed neighbors are typically southerner friendly.

The apartment fits Cassie's minimal needs at $230 per month. Which amounts to an average week's salary plus tips. Finding a place she can afford was a godsend. And it came with a big bonus in the form of a terrific landlord. But the location is what sold her. Walking distance to PJ's school. And within twenty minutes of the downtown club where she works as a bartender and part-time stripper.

Home at last, Cassie loosens a ponytail, shakes her hair free and kicks off the shiny, painful spikes. It takes her from a statuesque five-ten to a pettite five-four. She thinks, *De-glammed in seconds*. But this is one southern belle who will choose comfy over sexy every time.

She now stands barefoot, watching Lucas. He has finished stringing-up Christmas lights and is now sprawled out on the living room sofa. Sleeping and snoring so peacefully. She can't resist a playful toss with one of her shoes. Misses.Throws the other. This time, bull's-eye. A direct hit to an ample belly.

"Hey Luke, you big lug. Quit sleepin' on the job."

Lucas brushes the silver missle off his stomach. Sits up, groggy. Spots the cutie in the skimpy getup. And growls, "Y'all jus' loves messin' with me, dontcha?"

She gives him an impish smirk and nods. He comes back with a pointed finger and a laugh.

CHAPTER 2

Lucas Wilson is Cassie's seventy-eight year old landlord. He's also her handyman, babysitter and true friend. PJ was not old enough to be left alone at night, so kindly old Luke is a perfect fit. Widowed and living in the little house next door, he's always available. Best yet, he loves and treats PJ like a grandson.

It was Lucas who renovated the space over his garage for the rental income it could provide. His effort turned out to be fortunate for all concerned. Cassie and PJ were a most welcomed addition to a lonely life.

They're not just tenants. They're family.

Lucas is a short, stocky 200 pounder with a shaved head and a big smiley face. He's still a strong man. Plenty strong enough to push through the pain of the rheumatoid arthritis that has plagued him for so long. A third generation southerner, Luke has lived an entire, hard life in Florida.

Truth to tell, he never liked the label "black man". He's a man-in-full, period. Proud. Able. Honest. His father was born into slavery on a Georgian plantation in 1855 and took the surname Wilson from his owner. Emancipated ten years later, he moved to Florida and got work as a sharecropper. Unlike many, he worked long, hard hours. Raised a family of nine. Made sure they were fed, housed and clothed. Lucas feels that his heritage justifies his pride.

Now ready to leave for the night, he once again refuses payment for sitting Preston Jon. Cassie always offers. Always gets turned down. He knows how financially strapped she is. Especially with Christmas coming.

He angles his big, round head towards PJ's bedroom.

"PJ's in his pj's." Lucas gets his usual chuckle out of that one. "He's sound asleep. No doubt dreamin 'bout Santa." Smiles that kind, easy smile, "Brewed some decaf for y'all. It's sittin' on the stove. G'night missy. Sleep tight."

Cassie thanks dear old Luke. Gives him a big hug and a peck on the cheek. Her son and her landlord are two of the few comforts in her life.

CHAPTER 3

As Lucas leaves, Cassie goes to the bedroom. Kisses and tucks PJ in. He's named Preston after her famous granddaddy. And Jon after her father, an aviator war hero she never knew. The young mom now sits quietly, listening to her asthmatic son's labored breathing. So far, the enhalers are doing the job. But she worries that his condition might worsen. If that ever happened, how in the world would she pay the medical expenses?

She admonishes herself, *Stay strong. You'll find a way.*

Cassie thinks back to when she was PJ's age. She can't ignore the small voice, deep inside. The child's voice. To this day, she can't come to terms with what happened.

Sometimes she wonders about her own once-happy childhood. *Was it all an illusion?*

Leaving PJ's side, she undresses in the bathroom where Lucas has hung a full-length mirror. Turns a slow circle. As her own severest critic, she appraises the nude young woman standing before her. Pretty face. Same bone structure as Momma Abigail. Same complexion and hazel eyes. Natural blonde hair. Small waist. Great gams. Standing sideways now, she thrusts out a cutely prominent rear-end. Grinning at her anatomical profile, she muses, *You can sit a teacup on that tush.*

Cassie rates herself an eight plus. But still shy of a nine or ten. Not tall or busty enough. Just not hot enough. At least not compared to Blaze Starr and the other top showgirls who work the club. Which is why she's a bartender and only occasionally fills in as a stripper on amateur night.

Actually, she prefers it that way. Too much glamour is an open invitation to trouble. Sure, there's a fast way to make more money with her body. But she won't hook. Sex is now out of the question anyway. And for a good reason.

That reason took the form of crushing trauma at age fourteen. Try as she does, she knows it's something she'll never forget. Recurring nightmares ever since. *Rape will do that to you.* Thereafter, it took lots of prayers to help her accept the haunting episode as having a purpose. It gave her Preston Jon. That's purpose enough.

*   *   *

Cassie often contemplates, *Once upon a time, you had a dream life. Born into a super rich family. Lived on a grand estate in a white-columned mansion with servants. Pampered and privileged, with everything a child could want, including a loving momma and a legend of a granddaddy. Only one problem. It was a fairy tale without a happy ending.*

Since then, she calls her road traveled "Loser's Lane". It's a private, appropriate joke because she's lost so much along the way. First at age ten, it was granddaddy Preston and with him, their palatial home. Losses of childhood friends and schools followed. Then at fourteen, even her innocence was taken. Damned brutally, too. That's when she also lost her Momma Abigail so horribly. And if it all wasn't enough, just a year ago, her husband Tony...

Stop right there. Keep it together. Put him out of your head.

After removing makeup and showering, she slips into an old, comfortable chenille robe. Next stop, the kitchen for Luke's coffee. Finally, with cup in hand, to the living room, where she settles into a faded plaid sofa and turns on the TV. The sofa is actually a convertible bed she bought second-hand at a local consignment shop. It cost her $100. After the great buy she got on the used VW, it was her second best investment. She could now sleep in here, instead of the bedroom she had shared with PJ. Her unsettling dreams would no longer awaken him.

She drifts off, dozing through the final scenes of a Bogey & Bacall movie. The room is dark except for a dim, strobing light from the TV. Late evening programming has been over for at least an hour. It's almost 4 o'clock when she clicks off the set. Half awake, she surrenders to the memory. To Tony Roselli. To love. To marriage.

Cassie hears his thick Jersey accent, *"Fugedaboudit."* But she can't.

The year after was a blur of days for PJ and her. Only when the police finally closed the case, did both anger and hope start to subside. She has worked hard the past year to forget the hurt. Still, she thinks ruefully, *You keep comin' back like a song.*

A sad song. For a sad memory. She knows the lyrics to that Julie London tune, the one in her mind now, must have been written just for her. They are sung silently into slumber...

"In the wee small hours of the morning
While the whole wide world is fast asleep
You lie awake and think about the boy
And never ever think of counting sheep

When your lonely heart has learned its lesson
You'd be his if only he'd call
In the wee small hours of the morning
Thats the time you miss him most of all"

CHAPTER 4

In mid 1979, Cassie was nineteen. Tony was gorgeous. Black, curly hair. Square jaw. Tall and angular. She spots him as soon as he walks into "The Booby Trap" Club, heading straight for the bar she's tending. As he moves closer, he removes the sunglasses.

Oh, those big brown eyes. Let's go meet Mr. Italian Stallion. Her stilettos navigate to the far end of the bar where he now stands. He gives her a nice, easy smile over an open-collared silk shirt and some chest hair in which a St. Christopher medal nests.

Cassie takes in the whole package. *No wedding ring. But a big pinky diamond. Expensive haircut. Rollex watch. Catholic. St. Chris watching over him.* She thinks, *Looking like money.* Then wonders, *Money that fell off a truck?*

She leans over the bar. *Big smile plus big cleavage equals big tip.* "What'll you have?"

"Well, Miss Cassie Jean Dornwell, you can make it a Johnny Walker Black, up."

Her eyebrows arch. "Are you clairvoyant as well as good lookin'?

He gives her a faux serious frown, "Nope, just good lookin'." Then smiles broadly, "Manny gave me your name."

Manny Delgado is the big-hearted Cuban owner of The Booby Trap. He took Cassie under his wing three years ago. She told him how badly she needed the job. He felt sorry for the pretty kid. Especially when he heard she was a single mom with a kid of her own. She was only seventeen, but what the hell, with makeup could pass for older. She had a sweet smile and a fake ID, so he hired her. Then he "learned her" the bartending ropes. And has been her protector since. Manny wouldn't give a guy her name if he didn't know him and like him.

"Okay, you got mine." She grins, "What's yours? That is, besides Mr. Adonis."

Laughing, "Flattery gets you everything, including a really big tip. I'm Tony Roselli. From New Jersey. I saw you two days ago. You didn't see me. I asked Manny who that pretty, delicate little butterfly was. Just wanted to catch you in my net and put you in a jar to admire. But then I'd let you out... to come fly with me."

Cassie pours his scotch, knowing an outrageous line when she hears one. She slides the glass to Tony, "Thought I heard 'em all. But must admit, that butterfly thing is new."

He takes a quick sip. "Do you know the word for 'butterfly' in Italian?" When she shakes her head no, he draws the word out in a perfect accent, rolling the 'R'... MA-RI-PO-SA. He holds her eyes. "Mariposa. A beautiful word for a beautiful girl."

She returns an outlandish compliment with her very best southern belle smile, "Oh my, it gets even better. I don't believe a word you're sayin' but I do love hearin' it."

Tony laughs, "All in the Latin Lover tradition. Actually, I've been rehearsing the butterfly bit for two days. Did I get it right?" Now they're both laughing.

Cassie thinks it's a good beginning. *Just flirting, but who knows? Maybe he's the one. Maybe St. Chris will take care of me, too.*

For two weeks, Tony shows up at the club every night. Never watches the strippers or the shows. Just sits on his regular stool at the end of the bar, taking Cassie in. Grabbing small bits of conversation and sharing a smoke between the mixing and serving of drinks, and what little downtime she might have. Something's happening and they both know it.

When she ponders it later, *He had me at Mariposa. But it was the bar brawl that cinched it.*

It happened late that second week. Closing time at the club. Some big, blonde guy with huge arms full of tats started the fight. He was later identified as a linebacker for the Miami Dolphins. At almost 2 a.m., monster man is plastered. Loud, drunk, throwing his weight around. Cassie refuses to serve him a last drink. He calls her a "slutty bitch" and reaches over the bar for her. She thinks right away, *This is gonna get ugly.*

Tony stands between them and says, "Take it easy big guy. It's late and you've had enough."

Six-five, 250 pound pro player Billy Bob Wallace sizes Tony up and says, "Sit down pretty boy, before you get hurt. I don't like snotty whores and I like grease-ball wops even less."

Those are a lot of fighting words. Tony moves quickly. A short, hard left to the kidney bends the player at an odd angle, with his chin exposed. That first punch is followed by a right-cross, thrown with all of Tony's 180 pounds behind it. Billy Bob can feel his jaw break as he goes back over a bar stool and hits the floor. Tony is on him fast. Throws rapid lefts and rights to the head until the big line-backer is out cold. Other guys have to pull him off.

Manny Delgado gets there in time to see the end. He takes Tony aside and tells him, "Don't worry about it. He had it coming. You did good. That bastard's been a troublemaker around here for too long. I'll take care of everything. Get Cassie home safe."

Cassie is impressed. And grateful. That's quite a fella. But then within, a cautionary light goes on. *God a-mighty, he was ferocious. Is that the way they breed 'em in Jersey? Remind me to stay on his good side.*

After that, Tony starts picking her up at the garage apartment in the afternoon, drives her to work. Then home after. He never talks about himself. She gets little out of him except that he has no family and has "made a bundle in the stock market." Quite a man of mystery, but incredibly sweet and kind to her. Outlandish tips at the bar. Expensive presents and flowers. She hasn't been treated like this since her granddaddy spoiled her as a child.

Tony never makes an overtly sexual move. Long kisses good night. Hugs and smooches during the day. At times he can't resist playfully cupping that terrific tush. But that's it. He's a respectful gentleman. Seems fine with things the way they are. She's secretly ecstatic. After what happened six years ago, she's not quite ready for the next intimate step in a relationship. They spend many hours and when possible, days together. Taking PJ to Disney World, munching the treats, riding the rides, laughing and teasing each other. Like a real family.

*   *   *

Cassie has total recall of that special night. In her imagination, there was always a low Harvest Moon casting a soft orange glow on swaying palms. A light Fall breeze would be accompanied by a romantic guitar riffing in the background.

But that's not even close to the way it goes down. Instead, they are sitting in Tony's crimson Eldorado convertible with the top closing over their heads. Distant thunder and flashes of heat-lightning make that a wise move. Rain is coming and coming hard. It's like that in Florida. Heavy showers that leave as quickly as they arrive. Suddenly, a staccato burst on the windshield. Thereafter, they sit quietly. Eyes closed. Listening to the early-evening rain. Just enjoying the company while waiting out the weather.

Tony breaks the silence, "Look Cass, I know this started out as a lark. But now I'm dead serious. I think about us all the time. PJ too. He's such a great kid. And he can use a daddy. Hey, I'm thirty eight and tired of the bar scene. I want out of Jersey for good and I'm ready to settle down right here and now. Ready for a commitment. To you."

As a heavier rain pelts down around them, she takes his face in her hands and kisses him. A long, deep kiss. "I've never been proposed to before. Is that what this is?"

He nods in a good direction and more kisses follow.

Five days later they are standing before a Justice of the Peace in Orlando Town Hall. Manuel and Renee Delgado are witnesses. It's a spare, simple ceremony. PJ is the ring bearer. Lucas proudly gives the bride away. Cassie would have liked a bigger wedding and at least a mention in the local newspaper. But she's just as happy without any fanfare.

Besides, Tony insists on it. He's a private man with a lot to hide.

CHAPTER 5

Manny Delgado is in his office at 8 a.m., going over next month's bookings. He's got Blaze Starr and comic Redd Foxx locked-in. Good show. Reservations will be required.

One knotty-pine wall of his office is entirely occupied by a gun collection. He's got everything from a Colt 45 to an Uzi up there. Other walls are adorned with large, framed posters of star strippers. Tempest Storm, Georgia Southern, Sally Rand. Also black & white blowups of Robert Goulet, Joey Bishop, Don Rickles. His proudest trophy sits on his desk. A framed, autographed 8 x10 glossy of Sinatra and himself.

The office door is open a crack so he can hear if they are still working on the stage. A mechanic is fixing the overhead track from which red velvet curtains hang. An electrician is adjusting floods and strobes. Now he can also hear heavy footfalls coming his way. Without a knock, his door swings open. And there they are. The bigger of two gorillas flashes an NYPD shield. He takes a snapshot out of his jacket pocket and lays it on the desk.

"Tell dis guy we was lookin' for 'em."

A clear likeness of Tony Roselli. Manny shakes his head, "Never seen him before."

"Tink aboudit. When ya talk to 'em afta we leave, tell 'em we was here. Tell em we miss his company."

Without a blink Manny says, "I ain't talkin' to him." He hands the photo back, "Thats 'cause I don't know the guy. Check the other clubs around town."

"We did. He wun't go to no sleaze joints. Classy like your place is his style. Look, we know he's been heah. Been spotted makin nice-nice wit your blonde bartenda. We'll be back tomorra when your memory clears up. Capish?"

As they turn to leave Manny says, "Hey, next time knock."

Ape number two gets in a parting shot, "We figya da blonde broad is probly unda age. And who knows, maybe one of ya strippas shows too much t'night. Wud be a shame to lose ya license."

Manny says, "Hey, you got no jurisdiction here. But drop in sometime for a drink on the house. We're open 6 p.m. to 2 a.m. It's nice to make your acquaintance, though. Now get the fuck gone." They leave loudly, slamming the door hard enough to tilt Tempest Storm off-center.

When they've left, Manny dials Tony's cell phone. It's his honeymoon. He'll be on the boat.

Tony is in the galley having breakfast with Cassie when his cell rings. "Talk to me" he says cheerfully, scooping up some scrambled eggs.

It's a serious voice on the other end, "Listen up, T. Two big monkeys was here lookin' for you. Said they was cops but I make 'em for wiseguys. Said they'll be back tomorrow. They got nothin' from me. But you oughta know you've been made. Get ready for plan B, pal."

Tony moves away from Cassie into the salon area of a sixty-three foot modified Ocean Sport yacht. "Okay, got it. Looks like a shorter honeymoon. Thanks for the heads-up, amigo."

So far it's been a great two-week marriage. Good, unspoken things have passed between them. And there's plenty of pillow talk, too. She is completely forthcoming about her entire "Riches to Rags" life. The early joy. The heartache since, until now. Secretive Tony even shares more of himself. He's done things he's not proud of. At one time, fell in with the wrong crowd. They agree that with each other's help, they'll put the past behind them.

As to more intimate matters, Cassie forewarned Tony about the rape thing. He's been patient, considerate and gentle. He brings her around slowly. Around in fact, to her very first orgasm. She'd read about sex like this in romance novels. But her only prior experience with a man was brutally painful and shameful. Tony changed all that to something wonderful. Soft whispers of love. Touches and kisses to her newly receptive body. Gradually, every pent-up sexual frustration and emotion is released from within. *The butterfly floats.*

It's the real thing. Love as she's never known it, but always hoped it could be. For the first time in her life, Cassie truly feels like a woman. A woman born in this man's arms. She wants such a secure feeling of warmth and intimacy to last forever.

Unfortunately, there's just a day left in forever.

The honeymoon is over. Tony curses himself, *Dammit, how'd they make you? The yacht? The car? Traced the jewelry? You should have been less fucking arrogant. And more fucking careful. Always so sure you can stay ahead of them. Just when you find the right girl to start over with. And what about her now? Cassie deserves so much better.*

You are now a dead man walking. It's "endgame" time.

He shouts, "Cass, we gotta go. It's an emergency." He'll make up a reason later. There's an awful lot to do and not much time left. He climbs to the top deck and takes the wheel. The boat, christened "Cassie Jean" just weeks ago, turns and heads west for the Daytona Marina.

CHAPTER 6

On the way back to the dock, Tony tells Cassie the call was from his financial adviser. They have to meet ASAP. His endgame has five rehearsed phases. He now ponders the first two. *Settle her in their Hilton honeymoon suite. Then get to Lucas with some cash.*

Phase 1: They are back in their hotel room by noon. Just enough time left. He surreptitiously pockets his Glock, then packs a briefcase to show Cassie he's going to a business meeting. Tells her to order room service, probably won't be back for dinner. He holds her in his arms for a deep, lingering kiss. He says, "Stay put sweetheart. I'll call you later."

Then, a sobering thought, *Later? Or never?*

Phase 2: Tony drives to the garage apartment. That's where Lucas and PJ are watching a spring training game on TV. PJ says, "Luke, did you know that the New York Yankees are the best team in Baseball?" Another bite of popcorn, "And Mickey Mantle, who looked like he just stepped off a box of Wheaties, could hit the ball a 'country mile'!" Assuming that is literally true, he goes on, "When the season starts, dad's takin' me to a game at Yankee Stadium!"

Lucas smiles and teases, "Yo sure don't like yuh new daddy much, do yuh?" He hears a light tap on the kitchen door. It's the ninth inning of a close game. PJ never looks up while Luke goes to answer.

Tony motions him outside on the steps. Hands him a thick roll of bills. Cassie has told him about Lucas. He can be trusted. "This is to cover Cassie and PJ while I'm gone. Don't tell anybody about it. I have to leave on a business trip and want to make sure they're okay. I might not get back right away. Take good care of them."

Lucas frowns, "Y'all in some kinda trouble?"

"No, nothin' like that. Just a big business deal outta town. Look, I'm in a hurry. No time right now to say a proper goodbye to PJ. *Remember, this is just between you and me.*"

Lucas nods. Watches Tony scatter driveway gravel as he pulls out in the big crimson Caddy. Doesn't like the sound of this at all. But he's a man of his word and can keep a secret.

Endgame, Phase 3: A stop at South Orange Avenue. Tony's allowed just enough time, but gets stuck in cross town traffic and has to sweat it out. He gets to the Sun Trust just before 3 p.m. closing time. Makes an important, last minute transaction. *That was too close for comfort.*

Phase 4: Call Manny at the club. Review scenario. Then an afterthought, *One last drink with your buddy for old times. In case somebody's watching out front, use the rear stage exit.*

Big mistake.

Tony parks three blocks away and walks warily to the back side of The Booby Trap. Less than halfway there, a grey Ford Bronco pulls up. Two big guys in bright Bermuda shorts over white New Jersey legs, jump out and join him on the sidewalk. The one with the fashion faux pas black socks says, "You are so goin' down, Vince."

Tony's heart stops. Admonishment starts. *You arrogant asshole. Couldn't just settle for the phone call. You have to keep pushing the envelope, don't you?*

Black socks says, "Sloppy, Vince. Couldn't resist another *Red Eldorado*? It's like drivin' a fuckin' billboard that says 'here I am'."

They'd been cruising around casing the place all day, looking for the right car. He's cuffed and searched. His Glock is confiscated. He's thrown into the back of the Bronco. *Definitely not cops. Two upfront, one back with you. Him you recognize. A made man. One of Carmine's hitters, Benjy "Big Hurt" Esposito. Stay cool. Benjy will appreciate that.* Tony asks, "Where we headed?"

Big Hurt says, "No place ya really wanna go."

A call is made from the Bronco. "We got him. Should be there in ten minutes." Pretty good estimate. Eleven minutes later they're on the north side of town, in a sparsely populated, industrial-zoned area. They remote the garage door open and pull the Bronco inside. They're in a large, empty space. Hollow except for steel girders and two big leather desk chairs on casters.

Tony gets the scenario right away. One for the interrogator. *One for lucky ol' you.* At least the chairs look comfortable. He watches two of his abductors leave. Benjy sits him in one of the chairs with his hands still cuffed, then walks over to the nearest girder and leans against it. A good place to watch the show until he's ready to hold Tony down for the fun part. He shoves a Baretta into his belt and lights a Lucky. Tony asks, "Who we waiting for?"

Big Hurt is consistently short and sweet, "Nobody ya really wanna know."

That can mean only one thing... Sal, "The Answer Man" Rizzo. He's called that not because he gives answers. Because he gets them. He's Carmine's "quizzer", with a flawless interrogation record. *What an honor. The boss sends his best. All the way from Hells Kitchen, New York.*

The garage door opens again and closes. Speak of the devil. Here he is now, tool kit and all. Sal is a little weasel of a guy, known in Mafia circles as a paranoid sadist who never fails to get needed info. A small man who got his kicks bullying bigger men. Obviously relishing the task ahead, he gives his victim a tight smile. A nasal, whiney voice echos in the cavernous space. "I hope you don't make this too easy for me."

"Hi Sal. Still enjoyin' your work I see." *This guy's a certified psycho. A maniac who gets off on torture. You need a plan. Think, dammit!* Sal grins, "I'm told you got something belongs to Carmine. Over a mil, I

18

hear. How do you plan on spending it?"

Tony keeps his cool, "I'm thinkin' about givin' it to United Way."

Sal snickers, "Never had this pleasure with you, Vince. So let me give you the drill." Reaching into his kit, "Actually, it's not a drill. It's a set of pliers. You see my friend, your interrogation will be like pulling teeth." The guy can't resist bad puns. "So much fun for me, the dentist. So much agony for you, the patient. I know it's tough to talk without teeth, but you can always gum it." More yaks. He now grasps a branch cutter. "If you don't mind losing teeth, I'll take toes and fingers. One by one. Until The Answer Man gets answers."

Stall for time. Tony starts pleading his case, "Carmine's figured it all wrong, Sal." *Move fast*. "Let me explain." *Gotta be a surprise*.

Sal loves it when they beg. He stands arms folded, waiting. Amused.

Then a sudden, startling blur. Tony slams his heels to the concrete floor, propelling himself on casters towards Benji Big Hurt, still leaning on the girder, taking it all in. He is hit full force, chest high, banging his head hard against the steel support. Simultaneously, Tony slides out of the chair. His cuffed hands reach into Benjy's belt for the Baretta. He pulls the trigger. Blood explodes from Benjy's groin. Tony then turns quickly, firing twice.

The first shot catches Sal in the stomach. As he sinks to his knees, the second hits a shocked, then obliterated, face.

It took all of fifteen seconds. The only way it could possibly work.

Benjy Big Hurt is hurt big. But he's alive and passed out. Tony scrambles through his pockets for the cuff key. Finds it, frees his hands and climbs into the Bronco. *Thanks St. Chris, keys still in the ignition. Gotta get out of here before the other two come back*. He remotes the garage door open and steps on the accelerator, side-swiping Sal's Chrysler as he screeches out. The answer man won't be needing his Imperial anymore. Tony's mind races with his vehicle. Phase 5 next. End of the endgame.

CHAPTER 7

Tony heads straight for Daytona, about an hour away. The day is getting darker by the minute. He checks to see if anything is hanging in the rear view mirror that might be gaining on him. He watches blacktop and neighborhoods slide by for the last time. Finally, his headlights are stabbing through the chain link fence of the marina. He pulls up to the front gate and flashes his pass. *Linger. Show your ID. Engage him in conversation. Make sure you're remembered.*

He parks and boards the "Cassie Jean". Goes below deck to the bedroom. Sits wearily. The day is all over him as he writes a last letter to his bride. Packs it into a metalic waterproof safety box with his driver license and registration. Includes credit cards and a claim check from the cleaners. Three hundred in cash. Some personal jewelry. But he keeps St. Christopher around his neck.

Casting off the lines, Tony makes sure he leaves with lots of noise. The boat's fenders are banged up against pilings and bulkheads as he hits the throttle and pilots east into the Atlantic. When he reaches a lighted buoy close to the Florida Waterline Boundary, he cuts the engine.

Packs the bulging money belt around his waist. Takes off his clothes. Shouts, "Man overboard" and throws himself into a cold, black ocean.

*　　　　*　　　　*

Two days later, a frantic Cassie has called everyone she knows. Then the police. Manny Delgado is the only one who can help. He feels he has to tell both her and the cops about the wise guys who dropped into his place the day Tony went missing. On the third day an all-points is put out on Tony. Without success. Until a break comes from the Coast Guard.

His empty yacht has been found. Cassie is taken to the Orlando USCG Station where she's told by the Guard Commander that a thirty hour search was already on. Both rescue boats and choppers involved. He says, "Miss, I must be honest with you. The boat was a long way out. I've never known anyone to swim ashore from that distance."

Two weeks later, most of the dots have been connected. Detective Sergeant Michael "Gibby" Gibson is a thirty-five year vet of the Orlando PD. He's not a search guy. He's a homicide cop, looking well north of fifty. As a member of the CID (Criminal Investigations Division) he was an old hand at this. A kindly face and thick white hair makes for a fatherly demeanor. He's sitting with Cassie in the precinct house, updating her as gently as possible.

"Brace yourself hon. This won't be easy. On the day he left your hotel, your husband was abducted outside the club you work for. His car was found nearby. He subsequently escaped the garage he was taken to. Then left the same night to take out his boat. Two known Mafia men were found in that garage. Both are now dead. One was barely alive when found. He was still able to say, 'Vince got away'."

Cassie interrupts, "You do know his name is Tony?"

His answer takes her down hard. "I'm afraid not. Our investigation revealed he had a rap sheet in New York and New Jersey. His real name is Vincent Vega. He had a rep as a con artist and hot-head." Gibson frowns, "I have to ask. Did you ever see him get violent?"

Her eyes go distant, "Once. In the bar where I work. But the guy sure had it comin'."

"Figures. He served time for a few A & B's. That's Assault and Battery. Plus, the mob was after him for money he grifted from them. The rumor is it was over a million bucks. He headed south and took on a new identity. You know the rest."

As Cassie shudders, the detective puts a steadying hand on her shoulder, "For him, it was a very rough day and night. They might have worked him over in the garage before he killed them. No doubt in self-defense. After that, he made lotsa noise leaving the marina. Must have been disoriented. He either fell or jumped overboard. Based on his effects found on board, I'd say it was the latter." He shows her the metal box and opens it. "We must retain these contents for evidence until the case is closed. But you should read this letter he wrote to you."

She can hardly hold it steady enough...

Darling Cass,

Cant tell you how much it pains me to add more heartache to your life. I hope I at least gave you some happiness for a little while.

Honey, I fell in with some real bad people. Its all about money. This is the only way out. If I stayed alive they would hurt you and PJ to get to me and the money. They will only leave you alone if I am gone forever. By the time u read this, the cash will be with me at the bottom of the ocean. If anyone wants it, thats were they can find it. But its dirty money and now it wont cause anymore problems.

Go back to Luke. He will take care of you. Live your life and forget about me. But pray for me anyways. I can use it where im going. Give my love to PJ. Tell him Im sorry no yankee stadium.

I love you baby. Goodbye forever, Tony

Detective Michael "Gibby" Gibson can see the trembling lower lip between her teeth. She's gone distant again, eyes unfocused. *Poor kid. Younger than my own daughters. Fell for a wiseguy.* He hands her his card, "Be sure to call me if you ever need help."

She will. And under even worse circumstances.

CHAPTER 8

Cassie is swimming the Atlantic. From one end to the other. She's been at it for months. Or is it years? She has to find Tony.

At last, she's starting to get tired. She lets the tide carry her in. On the beach now, jogging.

Sand becomes asphalt. Jogging becomes running. Through streets that seem vaguely familiar. Old, rundown neighborhoods. Yes, that's it. Places moved into and out of while Momma Abigail searched for work. As she runs, Cassie passes schools attended. Friends made and lost along the way. She sees a street sign that says "Loser's Lane". She's running after her mother now. But not fast enough. Loses sight of dear Momma Abbey. Too soon.

It's now night. Somehow, she wanders onto an airport tarmac. Big commercial jets are landing and taking off all around her. She holds her hands over her ears to muffle the loud, whining noise of the jet engines. As an airliner passes by, she sees the pilot in the cockpit. It's her daddy Jon. Recognizes him from momma's photo albums. She starts running after him. Runs so fast that just like the wheels of his airliner, her feet liftoff the ground.

She can't believe it, but she's soaring like an eagle. Her daddy has flown away. But her own flight is an amazing, exhilarating sensation. The glow of Christmas lights and traffic can be seen below on a beautiful, starlit evening. There's a full moon, silver-white. To the left, the big dipper. And higher to the right... what in the world is that? It's looks like a sled. Being pulled by reindeer. Santa must be making his rounds. I'll have to tell PJ. Soon as I land.

The night fades into daybreak. She can see the sun making its appearance on the eastern horizon. Redder than Tony's Caddy. Spectacular. Soon, something even more glorious comes into view. Now she knows she's in heaven. It's as though she's an angel with a heavenly view of the place where she was born. She's moved by the beauty of a magnificent estate. There's the long drive that stretches from the front gates to a Tara-like mansion. The lush lawns and orchards that lie beyond. She sees the pool, big as a small lake. With its own waterfall. There's the tennis courts. The stables. The corral where her pony grazes.

It's called "Presthaven". Named for Preston Dylan Jennings, her beloved grandfather. Even at a very early age she sensed he was special. They called him a "tycoon". She wasn't sure what that meant, but knew it was important.

Cassie is now beaming brighter than the morning sun. Look, there's Momma Abbey. Wavin' to me. She looks so pretty in her big white hat. And there's nanny Gussie in her apron. And Willie, holdin' the limo door open for granddaddy Preston. He's standin' on the front porch, lookin' up at me. I can hear him shoutin' "Welcome Home Darlin'."

That's when an abrupt, shrill noise slams into her head. She's fetal. On her side, knees drawn up. Reaches out blindly, knocking over the bedside clock and silencing it. Groans for a while before finding a groggy voice, "Best goddam dream I've had in three years and the fuckin' alarm has to go off."

She looks up and sees PJ standing there in his pajamas, knuckles digging into sleepy eyes. Whoops. "Pretend darlin', that you didn't hear what momma just now said."

CHAPTER 9

It's minutes since the alarm went off. Monday, December twenty-second. Two days away from Christmas Eve, 1980. The day that will change Cassie's life forever.

PJ stands with hands on hips and a frustrated look on his freckled face, "It's cool mom, I hear worse in school. But hey, it's only eight o'clock. Did you forget it's Christmas week vacation?"

Cassie bolts up from the sofa bed. A look of disbelief, "Oh my God. And I was havin' such a wonderful dream. Could've slept hours more." She'd forgotten, alright. No need for the morning routine of getting PJ up and ready, fixing him breakfast, walking him to school.

No matter how late she got home from work, that was the self-imposed drill. Cassie was lucky to get four hours of sleep before the morning alarm went off. When she got in, she was too wound-up from the job to sleep. So she'd watch TV. Or work on her budget and think, *Your finances are going terminal. And cause of death will be self-inflicted.* By Christmas, she'll have a grand total of $25.50 in her account. Fifty cents over the minimum to write a check.

But she has the morning off and she'll put her flat-lining assets aside. Says to PJ, "Honey, you know the vacation routine. Momma gets sack time and you're on your own. First breakfast then next door with Luke or outside to play ball. You are my grown-up main man now. Am I right?"

"You're right, mom, I'm the man of the house. And I'm on vacation. Yipeee!" He leans over for a kiss. She gives him a big wet one.

It'll be pure luxury to lay around 'til mid afternoon before having to eat, dress and go to work. She's due at the Booby Trap by 6 p.m. But she'll get in early today. Prevail upon Manny to get her some fill-in strip time for better tips. *Meanwhile, think pleasant thoughts...*

She recalls the way mornings used to smell at Presthaven. Breakfast was prepared and served by her nanny Gussie. *Juices fresh from the grove. Shrimp and cheese grits. Biscuits and sausage gravy. Blueberry pancakes as big as the fryin' pan.*

Afterwards, the grand front porch becomes their classroom. *Swayin' on the glider with your books. Granddaddy Preston sittin' in his bentwood rocker with the lesson plans. You spend the first four hours on ''Readin', Writin' and 'Rithmetic. At noon, Gussie brings out lemonade and sandwiches. Then back to afternoon classes in History and Geography. Finally the part of home school you love the best. The last subjects of the day are what granddaddy calls "Life Lessons".*

They are vivid, enthralling tales of his amazingly full life. Both entertaining and educational. He tells her, "You've been given much in life, darlin'. I wasn't so lucky. I started out with nothing. So remember, it's not what you're given. It's what you make of whatever you have."

She was only seven years old, but never forgot those words. Wisdom (and genes) passed down. To survive what's coming, she's going to need all she can get.

CHAPTER 10

South Wales, United Kingdom, 1899.

With his tenth birthday just weeks away, Preston Dylan Jennings gets his first job. He works for a few shillings a day as a "dungboy". Hard labor for a youngster. In fact, for anybody. But he was grateful for it. Sometimes it was cold and the stuff he had to shovel would be frozen. Worse, if it was hot or rainy. Then it would get smelly and smeary. While he shovels away, he can always count on the other lads to taunt him.

"Ya missed some fookin' shite there dungboy." Egging each other on and laughing, "Better pick it up b'fore some bloke steps in it. Then you'll lose your fookin' high payin' job."

He just ignores them. But his twelve year old, fighting Irish girl friend next door, Betsy Hannigan, won't let them get away with it. "Your actin' like the horse's arses the dung comes from. Instead of runnin' your mouths, you should be working for your families like Preston."

That first job meant cleaning up and collecting horse manure off roads in the factory town of Aberdare. He'd shovel the foul stuff into a wagon and deliver it to local farmers for use as fertilizer.

As he got bigger and stronger, Preston got better jobs with shoemakers and blacksmiths. At age thirteen he advanced to the Blaenavon Iron Works. At Fourteen he was strong enough to go on to "Big Pit" and the mine. At sixteen he'd already survived a cave-in and was digging and hauling coal. A big lad for his age, he picked up extra shillings as a bare knuckle fighter in the pits. He gave as good, and mostly better, than he ever got.

Seventeen was the age he lost his virginity to Betsy Hannigan. And she to him. Since childhood, they'd been inseparable. But aside from that relationship, Preston's life was desperately unhappy. He lost his younger sister to tuberculosis; never enough heat, let alone medical treatment. His mum died in childbirth when she was twenty four. He lost his father, a life-long miner to lung disease a few years later. Preston watched him take a last, painful breath and pondered, *Life is so bloody unfair. You cannot spend the rest of yours here.*

Somehow he had to get out. To do so he must rely on prayer and a fierce inner drive for self-improvement. *You'll spend your spare time in the Aberdare Library. You'll educate yourself.* The problem was he had no time to spare. He worked six days a week, dawn to dusk. On the seventh, Sunday, the church was open for prayer. But the library was closed for education.

Betsy, as always, came to his rescue. She visited the ancient, two-story wood frame library on Front Street almost every day. Browsing through worn, moldy books. Waiting patiently for her opportunity. One afternoon when the librarian is back in the stacks, she quickly rummages through his desk, searching for a small treasure. Just as she hears his footsteps returning, she finds her objective in the left middle drawer. Snatching it, she silently closes the drawer just seconds before he arrives.

Preston hugs and kisses his dear Betsy like she's just given him all the keys to the kingdom. Even better. A single, stolen one that provides night entry into the library. Into hope, as well. From then on he spends months of all-nighters, reading voraciously. Self tutoring. Studying math. Working on English grammar. Improving his vocabulary.

One morning, just as the sun appears as a line of pink on the horizon, Preston has an epiphany. "The dawn of a new day" has never been so prophetic. Because that's when he discovers America. Finds her in a book on the back shelf. After that, he reads and re-reads everything he can find about "the land of opportunity." His chance for a better life. It's a chance he'll take.

*   *   *

December, 1910. They stand on a damp, frozen dock at Cardiff on the Bristol Channel that leads to the Atlantic Ocean. That's where the HMS Bounty is waiting to be boarded, steerage class. There is a difficult, tearful goodbye. Just Preston and a friend since childhood. Who also happens to be the love of his life. Betsy can't go with him. She has parents and siblings to take care of. There is sorrowful resentment in her voice as she says, "I wish I'd never given you that damned key. Why must you go, Pres?" But she knows why. For a year all he's talked about is America. By now it was his destiny.

Their knuckles are white from holding hands so tightly. She buries herself in his arms as he says, "I'll never want to let you go, Bets. It's a solemn promise. Soon as I get settled and can afford to pay your way, I'll send for you. We'll be together again. We'll have a better life."

He boards the Bounty, finds a rail on the lower deck from which to wave. Tears are freezing on both their faces as the big ship pulls away. Betsy is the last one left on the dock. Shivering. Watching Preston get smaller and smaller. Along with her life without him.

Neither yet knows she is pregnant with their child.

*   *   *

At age twenty, with a life savings of 151 pounds sterling in his boot, Preston arrives in New York Harbor. A worn-through coat is not enough against the chill as he passes through Immigration on Ellis Island. But he won't be shivering for long. He's studied his new country's geography and is familiar with it. It takes a month to hitch, hike and hobo his way south. The cold, black and white world of winter slowly disappears behind him. Warm, colorful Florida beckons, blooming with flora and opportunity. And as it gets even warmer, so do the people.

Preston finally settles down in a growing fishing village on the west coast. It's called Sarasota. That's where he starts his ascent from rags to riches.

By age twenty-one he's reached his full height of 6' 3" and is a ruggedly handsome young man. With his broad smile and charming

Welsh accent, he quickly wins over many new American friends. Men take an immediate liking to him. Women do too. Especially so. Within two years, he's built a "go-getter" reputation. His first job is in a general store with a single gas pump. It's located on a well-traveled road that later becomes "The Tamiami Trail" and Route 41. He also works a second job as night watchman for a boat storage facility on Siesta Key. Six months later, he's saved enough to gamble on an investment.

Although his youth in South Wales taught him frugality, Preston is also an instinctive entrepreneur. With a small deposit and a big mortgage, he buys 150 acres of cheap farmland that is quickly turned into a citrus grove. A big crop of oranges pays off his debt and returns a profit within thirty months. He immediately turns those profits into another, bigger grove. Then purchases the general store he first worked in and adds two more gas pumps. They are installed courtesy of the Texas Gulf Supply Company, newly formed as the result of a big oil strike in Texas. That was four years ago in 1910. The same year he arrived in America.

He remembers thinking, *A good omen*. And it was. The fledgling company later became the giant petroleum conglomerate, Gulf Oil. That early relationship would eventually take the young immigrant on a journey to unimagined success.

But in the meantime, Preston moves relentlessly forward. 1914 was the year Henry Ford revolutionized the automotive industry with a newly invented production line and the famous Model T. The age of mechanization had arrived. A year later, he buys his first Ford motor car. With it, signs a dealership contract to sell Fords in the recently booming town of Sarasota. Then he lease-purchases another Gulf gas station. He now has a small local monopoly, selling the newly available automobiles as well as the fuel that runs them.

His own entrepreneurial engine is hitting on all cylinders. But it is the next idea that will take him beyond rich.

CHAPTER 11

Like his contemporary, Tom Edison, who wintered in nearby Fort Myers, Preston needed and got, very little sleep. Compared to the back-breaking jobs in South Wales, getting rich by simply thinking and strategizing doesn't even qualify as work.

One January morning in 1920, just short of his thirtieth birthday, he gets *THE IDEA*. Like many revolutionary brainstorms, he wondered later why it was never thought of before.

The notion dawns in an unlikely place. Preston is sitting in his usual booth at his favorite eatery. It's a Longboat Key diner called "Elsie's Dry Dock". He likes the place for it's cozy, nautical decor. And for the equally warm waitress/owner in the sailor suit. Pale blue curtains filter sunlight through porthole shaped windows. Walls are colored gulf-blue, fish nets and buoys hang from the ceiling. Elsie, a widowed 65 year old with flame-tinted hair, always puts him in the corner booth. He's seated under a large picture of Douglas Fairbanks wearing a sea captain's hat. It's fitting. She thinks "Pres" looks like the swash-buckling film idol of the day.

Right now, her favorite customer is finishing his usual hearty breakfast. OJ, bacon and eggs, blueberry pancakes, coffee. Elsie adds to his cup and says, "Chilly mornin', ain't it Pres?"

Looking up from the Morning Herald, he smiles, "Sure is. Just reading today's high. Only 56. Still safe for the citrus, but guess it'll be sweater weather for awhile."

"More than a sweater" Elsie says, writing out his check, "it's in the

40's mid-state in Orlando where my daughter lives. And it's near freezin' upstate in Jacksonville.

Typically banal weather chat. Nonetheless, it switches on a light. A bright one. Sleepy brain cells are kicking back to life and getting seriously involved.

Cold. Heat. Midstate. Upstate. Preston's mind starts processing that simple data. Gulf Oil can do a helluva lot better than just gas stations. *Blimey! This is the way they can trump every petroleum company in the Florida home heating market.*

Mind gears are meshing. First, he needs a strategic mid-Florida location. His interest in citrus groves makes him aware of a semi-rural area just to the northwest of Orlando. The place is called Apopka. Centrally located. Land there is for sale at fifty cents an acre.

Preston, by age twenty-nine had already exceeded his goal of becoming a millionaire by thirty. He knows immediately what this new idea means: *Untold wealth. Many more millions.* The adrenalin is surging. He jumps out of the booth, spilling his coffee. Leaves the biggest tip Elsie ever got. In retrospect, a hundred bucks was not nearly enough. He is so wound-up, he kisses her on the way out. She wonders, *What in the hell brought that on?* She'll know in a month, when he returns to give her a bank check for ten times the tip.

*   *   *

Nothing beats the thrill of a great idea. Preston runs all the way from Elsie's Dry Dock to his office-apartment on Commonwealth Street. He rents the upper floor of the stately C.B. Wilson mansion. Wilson was President of the Saratoga First Bank & Trust. Like so many other locals, he'd taken a shine to the young Welshman and had already granted him some favorable loans.

Entering through the back door and staircase, he takes the steps two at a time. His place is a mess. Half bachelor pad and half untidy office. Various living essentials like clothes and left-over food containers are strewn around. Chairs that can't be sat in because they're full of cartons over-flowing with files. There are also some non-essential items. Liquor bottles, mostly empties. And recent souvenirs of romantic trysts. Largely in the form of feminine underwear.

He hurries through all of it to a cluttered desk. Reaching with one long arm, he sweeps debris, including a silk stocking, off the desktop, onto the floor. Setting to work now. Putting the business deal of a lifetime together. It's too early to phone Texas so he'll use the time for assembling logistics. First, he calls his real estate agent and puts a hold on a two hundred fifty acre parcel he knows of in Apopka. Then does the math. Works out distances to various areas of the state. Estimates construction costs for a fifty thousand square foot storage facility. By the time he finishes, it's almost 7 a.m. in Houston.

His intuition tells him to strike quickly. *Odds are against it. But it's a short cut worth taking. Beats hell out of waiting and wondering. It takes balls but you've got 'em. Make the damn call.*

Preston knows that the biggest brass are invariably the earliest in. He lifts the upright phone on his desk and dials the long distance operator. After a frustrating wait, he gives her a number he's surreptitiously obtained and stashed away. He hopes the boss' personal secretary won't be there to take the call. But if she is, he has a plan ready.

A sweet, slow western drawl answers, "Mr. Mellon's office. Who may ah say is callin'?"

Preston muffles and deepens his voice, "Tell him John D. Rockefeller." As hoped, the President of Standard Oil's name gets him through on only a few moment's hesitation.

The voice of William Larimer Mellon, founder and CEO of the Gulf Oil Company says, "Hello Johnny, how the hell are ya?"

Talk fast and think faster. He speaks as quickly and calmly as possible, "Mr. Mellon, this is not John D. I'm a business associate of your company in Florida. My name is Preston Dylan Jennings and I'm a bloke with a great idea that will make us both millions."

Click. Mellon hangs up and the line goes dead.

Just like the feeling in Preston's heart. More rehearsed words die in his throat. *Not good. This will now take lots of meetings and lots of time to get done. If ever. Dammit!*

Minutes later, the phone rings. Gulf's CEO has had second thoughts, "You've got three minutes to explain yourself. What's your big idea?"

Suddenly Preston's heart is drumming again. "I can tell you in a single sentence, sir... A Gulf Oil Company *Petroleum Storage and Distribution Center.*"

Preston's excitement is palpable, "It means fewer, larger deliveries of petrol that can be permanently stored. It means you can outmaneuver all your competitors who have to ship from out of state. From a centralized Florida location, fuel can be easily and economically distributed. It's a huge leg up on Standard Oil and everybody else."

He then goes through the details of his business plan. Right down to fuel storage capacities, market forecasts, distribution routes. Finally, bottom line cost and profit projections.

There is a long pause. Mellon says, "I know you're in Florida, but where from originally? I detect an accent."

"South Wales, sir."

"I thought so. I have friends in the coal business there. Good, hard working, honest people. I go largely on instinct, son. You've got a great idea there. And you know how to make it work. How soon can you get here to put this deal together?"

* * *

It took only two more weeks. When they signed all the contracts and then shook on it, William Larimer Mellon handed Preston Dylan Jennings his first check for $500,000. One percent of projected first year profits. With his percentage of the bottom line, he conservatively estimates his

34

wealth in ten years. By age forty, he will be worth a matching forty million.

It was time to call South Wales. He'd never met any girls in America as pretty, smart or loyal as his Betsy. If she still had family to take care of, that was fine. Now he could bring them all here.

There is to be one more family member that he was never told about. His daughter.

When naming her, Betsy kept Preston's surname intact. Abigail "Abbey" Jennings is a pretty ten year old who will soon arrive with her mom in America. Some day she will become Cassie Jean Dornwell's momma.

CHAPTER 12

December 24th, 1980. Ten in the morning. Enough time for Cassie to get to the bank before the noon closing in observance of Christmas. Next, Toys "R" Us and Sears for PJ's and Luke's last minute presents. Then home to them for dinner. The Booby Trap will be closed tonight. No work means no tips. With payday still a week away, that's not good.

Waiting in line for the teller, Cassie does the math as she writes her withdrawal slip. Her current assets total $75.50. Minus $50 for the presents, leaves her with $25.50. Thats exactly fifty cents more than First Federal's required minimum to qualify for a checking account. *PJ, my lil' man, looks like we'll be livin' on just tips 'n wits 'til next payday.*

Having worked her way to the front of the line, she passes her withdrawal slip under the teller's window. After counting out her cash, the teller's eyes widen as she sees the account balance receipt she now hands to her customer.

Wide eyes are nothing compared to Cassie's expression when she looks at it.

My God, what are all those zeros doin' there? No way. She returns the slip to the teller. "Bank error. This says, ONE MILLION and twenty-five fifty."

The teller, a very buttoned-up older woman, checks the account balance again. And again. She looks Cassie over. Young. Blonde. Pretty. With arched eyebrows she makes a facetious try at humor, "No mistake, dear. Perhaps there's a rich gentleman friend?"

Cassie reddens, "I don't even have a *poor gentleman* friend. What I do have, is a need to see the bank manager. As in right now!"

The teller, whose name tag reads "Karen O'Quinn" nods and puts a "closed" sign in her window. When two others, still standing in line protest, she says, "Sorry, emergency." Then to Cassie, "Come with me, dear." She thinks, *This will prove interesting. It's not every day a million dollars appears mysteriously in some paltry checking account.*

Inside the branch manager's office, curious head teller Karen introduces Cassie to her boss. Charles E. Thompson is an authoritative looking, world-weary man who thinks he's seen it all. The situation is explained to him. He smiles weakly and his manner is patronizing, "Well now, we have some diligence due on this, don't we Miss Dornwell? I'll be back shortly."

Cassie nods as her insides churn. "Due diligence" takes a full twenty minutes, which might as well be an eternity. Just when Cassie feels she's going to die of old age, Charles Thompson returns. This time with a much more solicitous smile for his latest wealthy client.

"Routing numbers check. Everything checks. The money was wired three days ago from The Bank of Switzerland." Now he *has* seen it all. "Congratulations, Miss Dornwell."

Cassie, who has been standing and fidgeting, slumps into a chair. Light-headed. Close to fainting. The same feeling she's had so many times before. But then it was always bad news. This couldn't be more different. *You now have a friggin' fortune in the bank. How can that be? A gift from God? If not Him, then who?*

She can barely stay contained. But good sense cautions her. This could be another fairy tale with an unhappy ending. That thought is seconded by Charles Thompson.

"Be prudent, young lady, I wouldn't spend it yet. We still have some bank follow-through to do and The United States Treasury Department will be interested in such a large deposit."

No, she won't spend it. Yet. *But just to know it's there is enough for now. A verified one million dollars in your name. And this time, no wake up alarm!*

It is an unexpectedly joyous Noel for Cassie Jean Dornwell. Tomorrow morning she, PJ and Lucas will exchange presents. She will say nothing to anyone about her own mystery gift. But tomorrow she'll still be wondering. Somebody knows she's poor and wants to make her rich. She can't stop asking herself, "Who?"

It's a question that will also be asked by others. And not just the U.S. Treasury. People with inside bank connections and long memories. Others from out of her past, present and future who will stop at nothing to take away her newly acquired fortune.

CHAPTER 13

Cassie welcomes the year 1981 with more optimism than she's had in a long time. Christmas also marked her 21st birthday and she is now better fixed financially than at any time since her marriage. And it wasn't just because of the mystery million dollar deposit, which she still hasn't counted as officially hers.

Right after the police close Tony's case as a suicide, Lucas invites her next door for "a cuppa joe". They sit in his kitchen, quietly commiserating. He reaches across the table and holds her hand. Gives some fatherly advice. Tells her to count on him now more than ever.

He also speaks of the day Tony went missing and his promise to keep a secret. "I'm still not givin' up hope on him, but I think it's time to tell yuh." He stands and reaches to the top shelf of his kitchen cabinet. "He lef' somethin' for yuh, missy. Said it was in case it took 'em a while to get back." Lucas hands her an antique, hand-painted cookie jar, "This here was lef' to me by mah momma. It's been good luck fo me. It's yurs now. And so's whut's in it. Money from Tony. Don't know how much. Figgerd it was yurs and I had no right countin' it."

Cassie nods and removes a thick wad of rolled-up bills. Her lips move in silence. Twenties, fifties, hundreds. When it's all counted out, she says to Luke, "Ten thousand memories."

*   *   *

A week of the new year goes by before Cassie gets a call back from the The First Federal branch manager, Charles Thompson. He tells her that a corporate officer will be contacting her about the anonymous deposit. She expresses concern but is told that the money is still secure in her name. Nothing to worry about, yet.

Yet? Two suspenseful weeks later, she gets another call from the bank. A fellow with a youthful, pleasant-sounding voice asks, "Is this Miss Cassie Jean Dornwell?" When he gets a yes, he tells her he's Harry McIntyre. A First Federal Vice President who would like to meet her. He says, "Just some technical stuff. Procedures we have to go through on all international wires. Let's make this pleasantly unofficial, shall we? Let me buy you lunch. We can chat about it there."

He's done his homework. Knows that Cassie is a looker and single. Wants to meet her for reasons beyond business. They agree on noon tomorrow, lunch at a place called "Cafe Two 2 Tango", a popular hangout not far from Disney World.

The next day, in her one-and-only sexy "civilian" outfit... big, white floppy hat, hot pink mini and matching high heels... Cassie walks into the small, colorful cafe.

A tall, baby-faced guy is waiting to greet her. "Hi. You must be Cassie Jean Dornwell. And I am... falling in love!" He chuckles, "Harry McIntyre here. Heard you were cute. Gross understatement."

Cassie thinks, *Spare me the line. Show me the money.*

Cafe Two 2 Tango proves to be a fun place. Modeled on a Spanish Loft, with rustic tables set around a curved mosaic bar. The ambiance is relaxing, with a soft guitar strumming in the background. Harry is as young and pleasant in person as his voice was on the phone. They sip Margaritas at the bar as she says, "Since when do banks have eighteen year old Vice Presidents?"

A good natured laugh, "I get that all the time. I'm twenty-nine, just look younger. From Boston. Graduated Harvard Business, got started with First Federal and fell into some luck last year. A VP had a heart attack and retired fast. The brass looked around for a replacement, and there I was. They know I'm young but I'm also smart. Up on all the regulations, auditing, technical stuff. Listen, what do you say we get business out of the way quickly. So we can talk about better, more important things." Cassie smiles, "What's better and more important than a million bucks in the bank?"

His response is fast, "When it's in the account of someone who *looks like a million bucks.*"

She ponders that, *Be careful. He sounds like another guy with a good, quick line. A guy you still haven't gotten over. A guy named Tony you loved with all your heart and always will.* "Well then, Mr. McIntyre, let's do talk business. I'm kinda anxious to know if that money is really mine for keeps."

He gives her an understanding nod and goes into procedural detail. Tells her that international money wires are automatically considered high risk. They must be guided by a "Bank Secrecy Anti Money-Laundering Act". Such an unusually high transfer as hers must be flagged and monitored. To be on the safe side, a Currency Transaction Report goes to the Treasury Department. Any suspicious activity connected with the transaction must be filed with Treasury's "Sin-Sen" unit.

Cassie reacts with, "Whew. You're makin' my lil' ol' head swim. That's a whole lot of procedure. Bottom line, please. When am I gonna know if that money's really mine?"

"It doesn't have to take too long. Doesn't even have to be filed with Treasury as 'suspicious activity'. Look Cassie, I'm on your side. Who wouldn't want to see a young girl down on her luck and after all you've been through, catch a break?"

"You seem to know a lot about me. How come?"

Harry smiles, "We are talking about a million dollars here, hon. I do my homework. You have been thoroughly vetted." Then says, "I don't want this to sound like a come-on, but I'm in a position to help you. I intend to. And with no strings attached."

Cassie is naturally suspicious. *He's a sharp guy. Could just be after what other sharp guys are usually after. But guess there's no harm in keepin' on his good side.* She smiles, "I like what you're sayin'. And I hope you can make it happen. Now, what else is there to talk about?"

He says, "A date for Saturday night."

She gives him a wink, "Thought you'd never ask."

After lunch, Harry pays the check and leaves over twenty percent. Cassie takes that in. She's a girl who works for tips and is always interested in how generous a guy is. They stroll out to the parking lot. He opens the VW door and watches her body fold into the front seat. He thinks, *Legs to die for.* But he says, "Who knows, Cassie Jean? One of these days, maybe you'll be driving a nice, big new car."

He watches her pull out onto International Drive. Then climbs into his Mercedes 350 SDL. Picks up his cell. Calls New York City. And says, "I'm on it".

CHAPTER 14

Cassie Jean Dornwell and Harry Miles McIntyre have been seeing each other for a month. They have good times together. It's her first involvement since Tony and she's finally enjoying some male companionship. Both are big into music and have fun singing to each other.

His song to her is a hit of the day, "Little Jeanie" by Elton John, "There were others who would treat you cruel. But oh Cassie Jeanie, I will always be your fool."

She does her best Judy Garland for him, "He's sweet as chocolate candy. Or honey from a bee. I'm just wild about Harry. And Harry's wild about me."

And since he's so doggone young looking, she also sings, "You got my heart a-jumpin'. You sure have started somethin'. You got the cutest little 'Baby Face'."

It's been over a year since Tony vanished and she's spent any time with a man. Especially one who obviously enjoys her company and cares for her welfare. She's getting good vibes from Harry. Even when he's mixing business with pleasure. He asks a lot about Tony, ostensibly to see if she's still hung-up on him. And wants to know if she has any idea who might have wired the money from Switzerland. She does have an idea. But will share it with no one.

As far as Harry is concerned, he's a professional with a job to do. But this new, increasingly personal relationship has caused conflicting feelings from deep within.

Looking into Cassie's eyes he thinks, *Dammit, don't fall for her. It will ruin everything.*

And when she looks into his, *It's not love. But it's a lot of "like".*

They are closer in age than she and Tony were. An eighteen year difference then. Harry is twenty-nine, Cassie's twenty-one. When they discuss their lives, he says his can't compare to hers for excitement. Her comment on that, "I'd prefer less excitement and more security."

He says, "The million will give you security. And I'll make sure you get it."

In reality, Harry's life is plenty exciting too. But his cover story is well prepared. "I'm just kind of a dull, nerdy guy. Raised in Cambridge and Back Bay, Boston. A big Red 'Sawx' fan. A book worm. Won a scholarship to Harvard. After graduation, recruited by First Federal. You know the rest. Except for one thing."

His eyes are now holding hers, "I met a girl I'm falling in love with." He says it while thinking, *And honey, that's not part of the con.*

*   *   *

After dropping Cassie off, he recalls her reaction. She was stunned. Took a while to compose herself. Then said only, "You have to give us both more time." After that, he drove her home in silence. But a long good-night kiss gave him renewed hope.

Now he arrives at his own residence. Quite a contrast to Cassie's garage apartment. This is a fourteenth floor suite in the high-rise Waldorf Astoria, Orlando. Very impressive. And well beyond the means of a young banker. Which is why he's been so secretive with everyone about where he lives. But his boss knows.

As soon as he steps into his spacious entrance foyer, he realizes he's not alone. A tough looking heavyweight stands at his built-in glass bar mixing a drink. And a short, stout, older man is out on the balcony smoking a cigar. Looking down at a spectacular, night-lighted pool.

Checking his buffed fingernails, he turns to Harry and says, "Hello Baby Face. You got a nice bachelor pad here. Ain't you glad you work for me and can afford it? Bet this place gets you laid a lot."

"Carmine. To what do I owe the pleasure?"

"You know fucking well to what. You're in that bank for a reason. I keep getting your bullshit 'progress reports'. But that don't give me Vince Vega and the million plus he stole."

This is a serious visit. Harry knows Carmine Battaglia, the New Jersey Cosa Nostra Capo doesn't like to travel. Harry's worked for him before and his previous investigations had been quite successful. Which is why he's so well paid.

Carmine goes on an increasingly intense tirade, "Vega owes me more than money. He offed two family guys. That's why I'm here in person. It's payback time. No more fuckups. I don't give a shit if the cops called it suicide. I know the muthafuckah's not dead. He'd never part with that kinda stash. I want the dough and I want him. You got one week to get me what I want."

Harry tries to reason with his boss while covering for Cassie, "Carmine, listen to me. By now, Vince is long-gone fish food. The girl's grandfather was a goddam tycoon. He could have left it to her when he died. It might have got lost and just turned up."

Carmine sneers, "I don't believe a word a that. Neither do you. You got a week to deliver."

Before leaving, Carmine feels the need to provide a little more Mafia motivation... "By the way, that's a nice view you got from the balcony. Be careful out there. It's a long way down."

CHAPTER 15

When the Stock Market crashed in 1929, Preston was well on his way to a tier of wealth equal to Joseph Kennedy and second only to such luminaries as Rockefeller, Mellon, Carnegie and Vanderbilt.

He lost much of that wealth in the market. But so did they. And he was still very well-fixed. More than rich enough in fact, to build his own dream mansion on a fabulous 100 acre estate in Apopka. It became renowned as "Presthaven".

By now Apopka was becoming a full-fledged town, building fast around the Gulf Oil Storage and Distribution Center brought there by the young Welshman.

Also by now, Betsy and he were married and their daughter Abbey was a beautiful almost eighteen year old debutante and student at Florida State University. They were the only ones in Betsy's family to take advantage of Preston's offer to live in America. Her parents were too old to travel and her siblings too well-settled in the old country.

The plantation-like Presthaven was completed in 1932. Its creator often asked himself, *Why so much house for so little family?* Then he'd think, *Why the hell not? You've come a long way and you're a wealthy man. Live like it!*

*   *   *

On a fine May day, Preston Dylan Jennings drives his latest toy, a 1934 Rolls Royce Phantom convertible through the gateway of his estate. From there, it's a half mile through rows of Magnolia and Banyan trees to

46

the circular drive that fronts the mansion. Stepping out of his new luxury import, he thinks he recognizes another vehicle that is just departing. It looks like Doc Williams' green Oldsmobile.

He crosses a grand front porch to a glass door etched with his Welsh Family Crest. Betsy is waiting in the vestibule with a kiss, her husband's favorite on-arrival Cutty Sark and a forced smile. He loosens his tie as they retire to the cozy, sun-dappled sitting room. It's their favorite place in the house, decorated by Betsy in soft colors and informal country furniture. This late afternoon starts like so many others. They often talk about South Wales, then and now. Or about Apopka and how his day went. Or about how Abbey is doing in college.

The latter discussion will make tonight different.

Betsy holds a Southern Comfort Manhattan in an unsteady hand, "Pres, I have something to tell you. You're not going to like it."

That gets his attention. He sets his glass down and sits forward, waiting for the worst. That's pretty much what he gets.

Betsy's soft hazel eyes are wet, "Abbey's upstairs crying. She got herself in trouble with a boy at FSU. Came home sick." With tears now, "She's preggers".

"I don't believe it! Are you sure?" Then he remembers the green Olds. *That was Doc Williams alright. No doubt confirming the bad news.*

Trying to deflect his anger, Betsy opts for sympathy, "Please go comfort her, Pres. She's upstairs crying her eyes out."

He takes the long curving staircase to his daughter's bedroom. Hears her sobbing and knocks loudly on the door. Abbey opens it and throws herself into his arms, "I'm so sorry, daddy. Please don't hate me."

His heart melts, "Do you love him?" When she nods yes, "Don't worry then, baby. What's his name? Daddy will fix everything."

Preston immediately makes several calls to insider connections and investigates the culprit. His name is Russell Underwood. No criminal record. A law student at FSU. On a four year scholarship. Extraordinarily high IQ with grades to match. Eighteen, only slightly older than Abbey, but a senior already. Good earnings potential. Middle class parentage. Too young to have much more background. If Abbey is so sure she's in love, what Preston now knows will have to do.

The man with a reputation for fast action is on the phone an hour later. He calls Florida State University in Gainsville and locates his quarry in a Bryan Hall dorm. Russell Underwood is read the riot act. His parents are next. The Underwood family is well aware of the multi-millionaire who has become famous all over Florida as a mover and shaker with a fast temper. They are quick to agree to a shotgun wedding. It's planned for June twentieth, less than two months from now. Before Abbey begins to "show".

When it's all settled, Russell Underwood congratulates himself. *Perfect fucking makes it fucking perfect. You are now a social-climbing member of a prominent, wealthy family. And an heir to the Jennings' fortune.*

CHAPTER 16

A hasty but nonetheless memorable wedding is arranged by Betsy. Naturally, it takes place at Presthaven. The beautiful mansion is a backdrop for an elaborate lawn ceremony. Abbey is typically vivacious. Russell typically taciturn. Everyone who is anyone attends. One notable exception is President Hoover, who is too busy trying to get re-elected. But otherwise, from politicians to movie stars, from international rich to local poor, hundreds are lavishly entertained. Preston is especially delighted to get re-acquainted with two of his guests. One is William Larimer Mellon, who launched him towards true wealth. The other is the person who unwittingly inspired a big idea: Elsie, the proprietress of "Elsie's Dry Dock".

The party goes well into the night, ending with a spectacular display of fireworks. It's a wedding to be remembered. But unfortunately, a marriage to be quickly forgotten.

From the outset, Preston had problems "getting" his new son-in-law. Too often he seemed sullen and remote, putting on a good face only when he had to. It was that remoteness that first attracted Abbey. He seemed so shy and mysterious. He'd sit alone in the library. Or by himself in the back row of lecture halls. He had a skyrocket IQ. Got exceptionally high grades in everything. Became known on campus as either "The Boy Genius", or "The Lone Stranger."

Opposites often attract. Abbey was a popular freshman with lots of friends. But Russell was different, a hard-to-get loner, an eighteen year old prodigy in his senior year. She had to ask him on their first date. They went steady thereafter. She found him attractively mysterious and "deep".

Russell was a deep thinker, alright. But he also had deep-seeded psychological issues. Raised in an environment of domestic stress, he lived in fear of morally corrupt parents and a physically abusive father. Russell was swimming in that same turbulent gene pool. When the mask of quiet calm dropped off, a terrible temperament was revealed.

In September, he graduated Summa Cum Laude and would return for a Masters Degree in Law. Abbey was also eighteen, but far more socially well-adjusted. A week later, both were delighted to move from their campus dorms to the luxury of Presthaven.

*   *   *

It takes months for Betsy to notice the bruises. Russell is careful about where he inflicts spousal punishment. The marks can only be seen when Abbey is in her bathing suit, sunning by the pool. She passes them off as a fall from her horse. But when more appear the next time mother and daughter swim, Betsy gets suspicious.

Knowing her husband's own short fuse, she's reluctant to tell Preston. After all, there's a marriage at stake here, and Preston's prone to hit first and talk later. But at least he only hits men. She recalls those days in the Welsh Coalfields when he fought bare-knuckled for money. And after that, for free. In tavern brawls. As he said, "Just for the fookin' fun of it".

Betsy will forever regret not telling Preston of her suspicions prior to her daughter's "accidental" fall one morning. It was just before Russell stalked out of the house in a rage.

Abbey is rushed to the hospital in great pain, both physical and mental. She knows well before she arrives and is examined, that the child carried in her womb has been lost. Meanwhile, Russell has disappeared, oblivious to the tragedy. Betsy now knows it's time to end the marriage. She calls Preston at his office to tell him what happened. He's told Abbey is in good care now but to find Russell and "let him know about it".

Preston is now raging, "I'll find him and let him know alright!" He rushes home with only one thing in mind... violent retribution for what's been done to his daughter and future grandchild. He looks first to his son-

50

in-law's favorite solitary activity, horseback riding on the back twenty acres of Presthaven.

Russell saves him the search. He's finished riding and is tying his horse to a corral post when he sees Preston striding towards him, fists tight at his side, knuckles white. He's not yet aware of the serious consequences of a punch that sent Abbey to the floor, but does recognize that look of rage on a father's face. He remembers the beatings. Something inside snaps. *You've taken enough of this shit from fucking patriarchs. You're as big as him and twenty plus years younger.*

He points his riding crop, "Don't even think about it, old man. You may rule this roost, but not me. When your spoiled little bitch gets out of hand, she needs to be taught respect." Now losing it completely, "And so do you!" He slams the crop down with a fury born of parental hate. It hits Preston's forehead with full force, opening a deep, bloody gash.

Preston drops to his knees, stunned by the force of the blow. He is immediately hit with a series of punishing rights and lefts to the head and body. As he goes fetal, rolling on his side to protect himself, Russell kicks him with spurred boots. Through flashes of pain, he manages to tackle the younger man's legs and bring him down. They roll through the dirt and mud of the corral and Preston thinks, *Now it's your kind of fight. Rough and tumble. Bare knuckles.*

From that point on, it's no contest. Russell is beaten nearly senseless. He ends up begging for mercy. There will be none. He's grabbed by his collar and dragged, bloody and with missing teeth, back to the mansion. He's given five minutes to pack and get out. Presthaven staff and workers are witnesses. It's a humiliation Russell Underwood will never forget. His sick, brilliant mind churns, *That bastard will pay for this. Some day. Somehow.*

The last they see of each other, Preston is shoving Russell into a waiting cab. Leaning in, he says, "You can go home to your parents now sonny. Divorce papers will follow. You're lucky I don't have you thrown in jail." His final words are spoken slowly for emphasis, "Go near Abigail again and I'll kill you with my own hands. That's a promise. And I've never made one I didn't keep."

CHAPTER 17

It's the day after Harry was given one more week by Carmine Battaglia. He fully understands the seriousness of that deadline. How he handles the next few days will make the difference between success and failure. In other words, life and death.

That same hot, humid day in a less elegant part of town, Lucas whistles his way to the corner mailboxes. That's where he usually sorts his and Cassie's deliveries. Then, as part of his morning exercise ritual, he climbs the garage stairs and slips her mail into the letter slot. He's thinking, *A good day for lil' missy. No bills.* Just a manila envelope with a lot of fancy-looking postage and "International Delivery" stamped in red.

An hour later, Cassie picks up the envelope with her address written in a familiar-looking scrawl. No return address. It's postmarked ten days earlier from Palermo, Italy. She tears it open quickly, simultaneously processing its possible meaning. Inside is something that nearly stops her heart... a St. Christopher Medal.

*   *   *

At that moment, Harry Miles McIntyre is also thought-processing, *Six more days to stay alive. With some luck you can get out of this in half that time.* His biggest concern is Cassie and PJ. Obviously he's got to warn her without seeing her again. He'll have a tail on him from here on out. Best to stay put, don't even leave the apartment. *You're a pro. You've been in bad spots before. Time to work the phones and the computer.*

The computer first. He clicks on the Treasury Department's private coded site. Bingo. What he's been working on for six weeks... approval of the deposit. The million has cleared. For all intents and purposes, it's now Cassie's. Some good news to go with the bad.

He then clicks on Trans World Airlines and books an overseas flight out of Miami for three passengers, two days from now.

Next, he calls Cassie and says, "Sit down honey, this going to come as a shock."

Cassie is already in shock. It's been just minutes since she's opened that envelope, found the medal and then compared the handwritten address to Tony's farewell letter. They matched. He's alive! She can see him now in her mind's eye, *Mailing that medal from wherever the heck Palermo is in Italy.*

Her reverie is interrupted by the alarm in Harry's voice, "Honey, first let me tell you that I got your deposit through Treasury. The money is yours."

First, the arrival of St. Christopher. And now this. She's excited beyond words. So, in response to Harry, there are none for her to speak.

"Did you faint, Cassie? Please talk to me. There's more... very important and urgent."

"Sorry, Harry. I'm kinda speechless at the mo'. Thinkin' what a lucky day this is for me."

"Well honey, hold that thought. But I'm afraid what I now have to tell you will change your day. And your life, for that matter. Because yours, PJ's and mine are in serious trouble."

That sobers Cassie up in a hurry. Harry reviews the entire proceedings since the million was deposited. Yes, he worked for the Mafia but she changed his mind and his heart. As of now, he's off their payroll. "But I sent them progress reports. They know where you live. They'll stop at nothing to make you turn over that million." He tells her it's imperative they leave well before his one week deadline is up. "If they knew what I just told you, you're in immediate trouble. And, unlike Vince Vega, alias

Tony Roselli, I'm dead."

Cassie catches her breath. *They know Tony's alive.*

Harry tells her to start packing. "I've booked reservations to Europe. Pack only for carry-ons. I'll buy what you need when we get there. We meet at the airport day after tomorrow. I'll call back with details." He tries for something positive, "You're going to love Paris, baby."

Cassie knows she's now swimming in deep water. How would granddaddy Preston keep her from drowning? *Collect your thoughts. Reason it through. If they know Tony's alive, then they know the money is still in play. Harry's right, they'll stop at nothing to get it. At the moment, Harry's your best hope. When you get to France, at least you'll be closer to Italy. And Tony.*

Her first concern is for PJ's asthmatic condition. She makes sure she assembles the required medication. Inhalers and prescriptions. "Albuterol", a "rescue" drug is a must. And "Symbicort" for preventative control. Then she packs the rest of their essentials.

While packing, she says to herself, *Granddaddy would say plan, but keep it simple.* She remembers a trick question he once asked her, "Do you know how to make God laugh?" When she shook no, he gave her the answer, *"Tell Him about all your fancy plans for the future."*

More good advise from the past. Especially with what happens next across town.

*　　　　*　　　　*

Harry stays holed-up in his apartment. Orders room service for meals. Spends most of his time making calls and arrangements for a safe departure. It's now 1 a.m. and he's tired. Only when he feels every detail has been covered for his rendezvous with Cassie and PJ at Miami International, does he get some needed sleep.

An hour later, he doesn't hear the small serrated blade picking his door lock. (Otherwise known to burglars as a "Master Key".) Nor does he hear the shoeless footsteps to his bedroom. They're on him even before he can reach the semi-automatic under his pillow. Two of them. Big, wrestler-built guys, the usual suspects for this kind of work. One of them was tending bar for Carmine during his visit a few days ago. For some careless reason, Harry assumed a fancy hotel like the Waldorf would have tighter security. But even without a so called master key, house dicks can be bribed for passkeys. And door latches can be silently removed by pros.

Harry, spooked and wide-eyed, tries to stay calm, "What's up, fellas? Carmine said I had a week. It's not even two days."

The bartender shrugs, "Things change. I heard you was such a smart guy. Did it ever occur that while we was waitin' for you to get home the other night, I might've tapped your phone? That's even easier than tailin' you all over town. From what we heard on those calls to your chippie, the little head is rulin' the big head. That gets you horny... and stupid."

Harry tries a desperate plea, "Listen fellas, Carmine doesn't have to know. I got dough... I can take good care of you. Just spare me the car ride."

The second thug grins, "Not to worry Harry, you ain't goin' for no car ride." The grin gets wider, "You're gonna fly."

What that means dawns on Harry just as he's injected and paralyzed. After all, Carmine made a promise that must be honored.

He can't move but knows very well what's happening. They carry him out to his balcony. He's thrown off, wide-eyed, facing death as it rises up to meet him. Lands with a sickening thud on the marble pool deck, fourteen floors below. D.O.A.

CHAPTER 18

At 2 a.m., the Orlando Waldorf Astoria Hotel grounds are lit-up like DisneyWorld. The place is alive with patrol cars parked at odd angles, flashing lights, an ambulance, remote TV crews. And curious people.

OPD Homicide Detective Sergeant Michael "Gibby" Gibson has just arrived in his unmarked Dodge Charger with a rooftop blue-flasher that adds to the festivities. Crowds of crane-necked onlookers watch as he walks past the yellow crime scene tapes to the center of attraction... what used to be Harry Miles McIntyre. Arms and legs at odd angles. Insides out. He twisted as he fell, landing on his back. So Harry's bloody baby face is still recognizable.

An officer under Gibson's command is crouching over the body. His name is Dwayne "Sonny" Lang, out of the Chicago PD. He looks up at his boss, "A mob whack for sure, sarge. This is the same guy you've had me watchin' for the past month."

Gibby had ordered surveillance on Harry since he started going with Cassie. Vince Vega may or may not have jumped and drowned in the ocean, but the detective doubted the money went with him. The police, like the Mafia, knew about the big deposit in Cassie's account and figured it was from Vega. Besides, Gibson had taken a personal interest in her safety.

Officer Lang gives his boss a rueful smile, "Guys who go out with that babe seem to fall for her, don't they?"

Gibby just shakes his head, "Not funny, Sonny." He frowns, "She's a good kid and awful young. I got a badge that's fifteen years older. She

56

and her kid are gonna need us."

*   *   *

The "Waldorf Jumper" is worth a two column headline in the Saturday morning edition of the Orlando Sentinel. Cassie cannot believe what she's read or what she's now watching on TV. Anchor man Paul Alvarez is reporting from the scene. With Detective Sergeant Michael Gibson's card in her hand and her heart in her mouth, she's on the phone. Gibby picks up and hears a panicky plea, "You said to call if I ever needed your help. I need it now!"

He recognizes the voice and tries to calm her down, "What, not even a hello? Or a how's the family, Gibby?"

She's in no mood for calm, "The morning paper and the TV says the jumper has been identified as Harold Miles McIntyre." Her voice is unable to disguise the fear, "Is it true?"

Gibby says, "I'm afraid it is. And he was no jumper. More like thrown-out mob garbage. Your Harry was Mafia connected, just like Vincent Vega. You do have to be more careful about picking your friends. And you do need help. If you look out your window, you'll see that it's already arrived."

Cassie moves a curtain aside and looks down to a patrol car in the garage driveway. Tension is coming off her in waves, "Where are these Mafia guys at?" How much trouble am I in?"

The veteran sergeant attempts to lighten things up, "Shame on you darlin', you just ended two sentences in prepositions." Then his voice shifts to reassuring, "You and your son will be fine. You'll be under steady guard until we find you a safe place to stay. Look hon, you're like a daughter to me. From here on out, I'm gonna take good care of you and your boy."

Since there's no school today, PJ is next door at Lucas' house. Cassie joins them. Preston Jon excitedly tells his mother, "This is so cool. There's a cop car in the driveway. Luke says it's there for us. How come, mom?"

57

Cassie does her best to explain things to a child still shy of his ninth birthday. She tells him that the same bad guys who were after daddy Tony may now be looking for them. But everything's good. The police and Lucas will protect them.

Her landlord chimes in, "Y'all gonna be stayin' with ol' Luke. Mo' room in mah house for a policeman to be right in here with us. Plus I got mah own shotgun ready fer trouble."

It sounds like a plan. At least until Mike Gibson is able to locate better refuge. She informs him of their new temporary living quarters and gets his approval. Then she calls Manny, best friend of Tony and her benefactor since she was a seventeen year old in need of a job.

Manny listens to the situation and gives her reassurance. He says PJ is safe with Lucas and the cops tonight. And she'll be safe at the Booby Trap with him and big Joey G, the Club's bouncer. He'll have cops there too, just to make sure. He says, "Come in for tonight only Cass. I want to see you before the cops stash you away. Get all dolled up and work the bar one last time. I got a nice bonus set aside for you. Joey G will pick you up and take you home. He's licenced to carry a weapon. I'm an old buddy of Mike Gibson. I'll give him a heads-up."

Cassie trusts Manny implicitly. She agrees to come in, but only if he gets the okay from Sergeant Gibson. Then she has a question, "Why did you let me think Tony was dead?"

There's a pause before Manny answers with another question, "Why do you think he's not?"

"Saint Christopher told me. You helped him get away, didn't you?"

"It was for your own safety, baby. Yeah, we had it worked out. It was the last step of the "endgame". After he jumped in the water, I had a guy waitin' in a skiff with some fresh clothes. They set their compasses to meet at a lighted buoy near the Florida Waterline Boundary. My guy picked him up and took him to the airport. Tony flew Alitalia straight to Rome."

CHAPTER 19

The Lucas house. Midnight. PJ is sleeping in the bedroom. Cassie has called from work four times since 6 p.m. Lucas and officer Dwayne "Sonny" Lang are playing Poker five-card-draw for fifty cents a hand. The old man is soporific and yawning. He's also down $5.50.

All windows and doors have been checked and secured by Lang, who volunteered for this duty as a follow-up to the McIntyre surveillance. Lang's partner is in the squad car parked in front of the house. It's part of Sergeant Gibson's 24 hour plan to have two officers on guard, one inside and one outside.

Now it's time for the midnight call check to Gibby. Lang says, "Everything is locked-down here, chief. Carson's out front where he can be seen and I'm in here with Lucas and the boy. No problems."

Gibby's voice is sleepy, "Good. Cassie should be home in a couple of hours. You guys will be relieved by the next team at that time."

"That's cool chief. No worries. Get some sack time."

Actually, Lang's partner Mitch Carson is sleeping soundly in their car out front. The cup of drugged coffee brought to him by Sonny has done the job. He'll be out for hours.

Now it's time for him to go to work in here. The sedatives he's been slipping Lucas are finally kicking-in. Lang thinks, *Fat sambo is on his way to La-La Land. Start prepping the place for the "break-in". Get this right, Sonny. It's the chance you've been waiting for all your life. A million dollar score.*

Lucas drifts into darkness, chin dropping to chest. The police officer then karate chops the back of Luke's thick neck. He won't wake for quite some time. And he'll hear nothing. That's important because some noise will be made while a forced entry is faked.

Dwayne Lang still can't believe this deal fell into his lap so easily.

He arrived in Orlando six years after graduating the Chicago Police Academy. He was always a step ahead of the gang in Cicero, Illinois, where he grew up. A street-smart kid with larceny forever in mind, he knew a cop's uniform would make it that much easier to break the laws he was sworn to uphold. He had five on-the-take years of graft, political kickbacks and drug dealer protection money. Chicago was a gold mine of corruption. But he and his mom tired of the harsh winters and winds off the lake. So at age twenty-eight, he got himself transferred to Florida on a hardship ruling. He was the sole support of an "anemic, ailing mother" who needed warm weather and sunshine to get well.

It was his good luck to get situated with Gibby in the OPD. The Detective Sergeant was looking for a tough, experienced officer. Especially one from up north with some mob experience. Then, when he was assigned to watch Harry McIntyre and the million dollar babe, his luck got exponentially better. That's when he started putting the kidnap plan together.

Now he was all set. Gibson would be looking for mob guys. The "Mafia" ransom note would say they grabbed the kid, and the cop too. He'd lay low and stash the kid with his mom at her "Senior Village" condo. She'd have to keep him under wraps for only a day. But if anybody saw him, he was her grandson. He'd let the kid loose after the million was wired to the Cayman Islands, where it couldn't be traced to him.

Lang goes to PJ, sleeping in the bedroom, and notices breathing that sounds labored. It's like the kid might have Bronchitis or something. But a little chloroform won't hurt him.

When that's done, he starts knocking over furniture. Breaks a lamp and drags Lucas to the floor. Goes to the rear of the house, jams open the back door from the outside and shatters glass. When he's satisfied it looks like a break-in and a struggle, he wraps an unconscious PJ in a blanket and carries him out the back way. Under cover of darkness, he puts him in an old Ford pickup that's parked a half block behind the house. Leaving his squad car parked out front with sleeping fellow officer Mitch Carson still in it, the cop turned kidnapper drives off into the night.

Dwayne Lang gives himself high marks so far. But there is something he's overlooked. And that's unfortunate. Not for him, for PJ.

He never noticed the items sitting on the night stand next to PJ's bed. Any excitement or unusual activity might make them mandatory to save a life. But the inhaler and even more importantly, the vial of Albuterol Sulfate pills, remained behind. Prescription only, for Asthma rescue.

CHAPTER 20

October, 1943. Jon Dornwell, the father Cassie never knew, is sweating out a midnight landing near Arnhem, Germany. He thinks to himself, *There it is... open ground. Set her down nice and easy.* In total darkness, he guides his glider to a quiet landing behind Nazi lines.

The big Waco CG-4A motorless craft is loaded with military personnel and equipment. It hits ground with minimal noise and damage. The squadron leader, a big Irishman named Sean Murphy nods, "Nice job, Jonny. Smooth as a baby's butt."

"All in a night's work, Murph." Another do-or-die, semi-crash landing for the young pilot.

Murphy unloads his men and their 2000 pound equipment cargo off the glider. When the entire unit is on the ground, he turns to his transporter, "Good luck gettin' back, Jonny."

Dornwell says, "Send me a telegram when you take out that kraut bunker." They shake hands. Jon always worries about the men he carries. But at least they have each other. Now, all on his own, he has to find and possibly fight his way back to the base.

With an AK-47 assault rifle, a sidearm, K rations, a map, a flashlight and a compass, he heads southwest. Hanging with the dog tags around his neck, is a St. Christopher medal. It's a safe-travel icon with which he never parts.

Jon Dornwell was an intrepid adrenalin addict. He thrived on risk and would have relished the odds his future daughter had to face forty years later. He was also a genuine American hero. One of an elite, unique squadron of aviators in World War 2. They had no motors, no parachutes and almost no second chances.

In 1944, after fulfilling his required number of missions in Europe, he visited Miami, Florida on a two week furlough. That's where he met Abigail "Abbey" Jennings. They fell quickly in love and married. Her daddy Preston and mom Betsy, both of whom preferred flamboyant weddings, were at first dismayed by the elopement with a stranger. Later, after Preston had the young man thoroughly investigated, they couldn't be happier. He'd made a trip to Washington DC and met with General Westmoreland. The General informed him of the young pilot's war record. Preston was thrilled to have such an outstanding young man in the family. His new son-in-law Jon Dornwell was everything his old one, Russell Underwood, was not.

*   *   *

Abbey met Jon on Key Biscayne, a vacation paradise minutes from downtown Miami. He had just arrived. She and some girlfriends were sitting with mimosas and conch chowders at a chickee hut just off Virginia Key Beach.

She noticed him through the chickee's umbrella of palm fronds... a handsome young man in an Air Force Lieutenant's uniform. Their eyes met. Something shifted inside Jon that he didn't quite understand. So he walked on. But they both knew that wasn't the end of it. She went back to the same chickee hut later that afternoon. He was waiting there.

They talked for hours. The sun was setting. It colored everything, including Abbey, in soft magenta hues. He was entranced by the sight of her. And the feeling was mutual. On warm white sands and under breezy Coconut Palms, they shared their past and present lives. And dreamed of a future together.

Some days they'd just sit and watch Southeast Florida go by. In the ocean were dolphins, sail boats and cruise ships. Surfers skimming waves that rushed towards the beach. In the sky, seagulls and pelicans, kites and frisbees. A small plane sky-writing, and for competition, the Goodyear

Blimp. They swam, sailed and scuba-dived. During their second week they discovered a beautiful little church just off Harbor Drive. Jon loved the name. He felt it was a good omen for a future together... "St. Christopher's By-The-Sea". They were quietly married there. It was an unobtrusive ceremony; the opposite of Abbey's first wedding to Russell. No Presthaven fireworks this time. Except for the ones they made on their own.

When WW 2 ended in 1945, Lieutenant Jon Dornwell remained on Reserve Command Duty. Many days with Abbey were happily spent in wonderful Presthaven. But he also flew them all over the world in the various aircraft he loved to pilot. It was an adventurous, near idyllic life. Except for one thing. They wanted children, but remained childless.

In 1958, their lives changed abruptly. Jon, now 42 years old, was called back to duty. Conditions were getting dangerous in Vietnam. Communist troops in the north were invading the South and threatening America's global interests during the Cold War. Men like Lieutenant Jon Dornwell, with both covert and combat war experience were needed to train our allies, the South Vietnamese Forces. The operation he took part in would remain secret. He was assigned to the USMAAG (U.S. Military Assistance Advisor Group), set up originally as a clandestine operation by President Eisenhower. It was not until years later that the American public became aware of the extent of their involvement in Vietnam.

All Abbey knew was that his mission was confidential and that he'd be back in a month or two. On a warm day in April, she drove Jon to the Patrick Air Force Base at Cocoa Beach for their farewell. As they stood on the tarmac embracing, he placed his St. Christopher medal in her palm and folded her hand over it. He whispered, "Stay safe, sweetheart. Until I get back."

It was three weeks after they parted that she got both wonderful and horrible news on the same day. In the morning, from her doctor. She was pregnant. That afternoon, from the USMAAG. Her husband was killed in a plane crash.

CHAPTER 21

Abigail Jennings Dornwell never knew the true value of the St. Christopher medal. It meant even more to her husband than the wedding ring he slipped on her finger that day in Key Biscayne. In Jon's mind, the medal was a proof of love. He'd put her safety before his own.

Abbey wasn't aware of the symbolism. If so, she'd have given the good saint right back. But medal or no medal, it was another adrenalin rush that got Lieutenant Jon Dornwell in trouble. On a reconn flight across the North Vietnam border, he flew at a dangerously low altitude to get a better look at enemy troop emplacements. As a result, he couldn't lift his F4 Phantom Jet fast enough to avoid the looming Ba Den mountain range.

The silver medal pressed into her palm was the last thing her husband ever gave her. Abbey carried it until she passed it on to Cassie years later.

Confident in a way she can never fully explain, Abbey knows the child within her was conceived on their last evening together. She can't get those wonderful years out of her mind, and often explores her photo album in search of memories. Jon in uniform. Waving from a cockpit. With her in that tiny arcade photo booth. On the Great Wall of China. At the Louvre Museum. The Grand Canyon. Family snapshots of Jon with a proud Momma Betsy and Daddy Preston. Images that will eventually become Cassie's only connection to her father.

Betsy and Preston mourn their son-in-law's death right along with daughter Abigail. They console each other through nine anxious months of waiting for a mid-life daughter to give birth. Finally, on Christmas day, 1958, she has her "miracle baby". The emergence of Cassie Jean

Dornwell takes the Jennings family out of darkness and into a bright and shiny new world.

*   *   *

Also in 1958, Abbey's first husband, Russell Underwood is now a successful forty-two year old attorney, the owner of a thriving law practice located in the state capital, Tallahassee. The brilliant Summa Cum Laude graduate of Florida State University has put a lot of distance between himself and his ex-father-in-law. But he never forgot the humiliation.

Always nice looking, he has matured into a handsome man, bulked-up from daily workouts, tanned and fit with thick, greying hair. Women find him attractive, making his extra-curricular life that much easier. He now wears the mask of respectability well. But extreme misogynistic behavior lurks behind it. Over time, he has advanced from miscellaneous attacks on women, starting with his wife Abigail, to much more serious crimes. Underwood is a Mensa Master with a genius IQ. He is also a split personality psychopath. A renowned trial lawyer. An unknown serial rapist/killer.

Only a super intellect could escape detection. It's been twenty-five years since he was thrown out of Presthaven and divorced from Abbey. Up to that time, he was the cause of just one fatality, his own child in his wife's womb. Preston Jennings' big mistake was not putting him away then. Because since then, the score is eleven to nothing. That is, eleven homicides to zero cases solved by the police.

His parents were the first victims. A physically abusive father who often pimped-out a whore wife. His mother Helen was the first woman he hated. Many more would follow. Arthur and Helen Underwood died at home in a fire set by their son. It was ruled accidental. Nine other killings were of women. Raped, then strangled or beaten to death.

Driven by revenge, he's not through yet. Preston Dylan Jennings will pay a heavy price for ending his marriage to Abbey, and by doing so, eliminating Russell as an heir to the Jennings fortune. He's sworn to take away what that bastard loves the most...

His wife, his daughter and his money.

66

CHAPTER 22

Russell Underwood was stunned. Just like all men and many women, when they saw her in person. On an appearance scale of one to ten, Cassie would have rated her an eleven.

She was standing in the doorway to his office, even more beautiful than so many of her pictures led him to believe. Six feet tall in a sheath dress that should have come with curve warnings. Lustrous auburn hair and green eyes to match a jade necklace that dipped into deep cleavage. Drop-dead gorgeous. A younger version of another extraordinary southern beauty, actress Ava Gardner.

The latter was probably in Spain, being pursued by bull fighters. But Savannah Lindstrom Murcer is right here, with even more notoriety. The senior partner of Underwood and Associates stands beside his impressive desk and tries not to stare. He holds a chair for her and starts with, "Newspapers, magazines and TV don't do you justice, Mrs. Murcer." Then with a slight smile, "And the recent notoriety doesn't either."

"Call me Savannah. I'm no longer Mrs. Murcer. My bastard husband is dead. The prick deserves to rot in hell. And fuck the notoriety."

Russell's smile broadens. He's going to like this famous and brutally outspoken woman. She's been all over every news media outlet for a solid week. Prior to that, Savannah Lindstrom was a minor actress and a well-known model. The close resemblance to Ava Gardner helped. It often misled TV viewers to think it was the actress herself, endorsing a product.

Now, she's in trouble. Her wealthy spouse was murdered last week

67

in Miami. The media immediately labeled her the number one suspect. A call quickly went out to Russell Underwood, who had established a reputation as the best trial lawyer in Florida.

Savannah asks, "Am I correct in assuming that everything said behind closed doors in this office is protected by client-attorney privilege?" Underwood confirms it. Then listens to an amazingly forthright diatribe, "I was too young and stupid to read the fine print when I married Ben Murcer. For the obvious reason, his money. But the dirt bag had an airtight pre-nup that I stupidly signed. If that wasn't enough, he was screwing every piece of ass within reach. He was a cheap, abusive fuck who deserved the bullet I gave him in his fat gut. He came home late, 3 a.m. It was dark. I was just protecting myself from an intruder. Right?"

Russell's eyebrows arch at such a candid description and implication.

However, he responds with legal assurance, "Please, say no more. I fully understand you had no choice but to defend yourself. I assume you've been informed by authorities of your rights and have been told not to leave the state." When she nods in affirmation, he says confidently, "No doubt there's a murder trial coming. Our defense will be 'justifiable homicide'. I'll have to get a change of venue. The notoriety in Miami will be prejudicial to your case".

He then predicts the result, "You needn't worry. I haven't the slightest doubt that my proficiency, along with a carefully selected jury, will have you found not guilty."

Savannah responds, "You're very sure of yourself, aren't you? I like that in a man. But there's now the question of your fee."

When he tells her, she shakes her head, "I can't afford that. Didn't you hear about the pre-nup? I haven't done any modeling since the marriage. And I sure won't be getting any more bookings, now." Then, a pause and a seductive smile, "Do you think we can work out some kind of mutually agreeable payment plan?"

As Russell thinks about that, she shows him a bent index finger. He moves to where she beckons. Still sitting, she motions him closer. Her beautiful face is now at belt level. A tongue slips over full, luscious lips. She looks up, holds his eyes and says, "Between now and the trial, how would you like to be payed?"

Russell Underwood the psychopath lawyer, even at such a wanton and enticing moment, is scheming...

This woman will make a perfect partner. A promiscuous, larcenous sociopath. A murderess already. Yes, Savannah Lindstrom will be of great assistance in separating Preston Dylan Jennings from his women and his fortune.

CHAPTER 23

Early morning, May 20th, 1982. Cassie, as only a mother can, sensed that something was terribly wrong even before she called Lucas at 1 a.m. and got no answer.

She runs quickly out of the club with Joey G in tow. They go ninety in a speed zone of fifty. The big club bouncer tries to reassure her everything will be okay. When they get off 408 and onto Oriovista, they hear a police siren, possibly a mile behind them. Cassie says, "Don't stop, maybe we can use them when we get there."

They zig-zag on two wheels onto Grove Street, where Luke lives. The police cruiser, with officer Mitch Carson in it, is still parked in front of the house. It's a momentarily welcomed sight. Except, the damn cop inside is sleeping! Cassie leaps out, running to the front door. It's locked. As she fumbles for her key, the pursuing squad car comes barreling in, spotters and light bars flashing, siren wailing.

Cassie pushes into the house with Joey G right behind, gun in hand. She screams when she sees Lucas still on the floor, unconscious. Her scream is louder when she rushes to the bedroom and finds PJ gone. And with his potentially life-saving vial of pills still sitting on the bed stand. She collapses.

The two cops chasing them are now in the house as well. One runs back to the car and radios for assistance. He says, "Looks like a break-in. And a possible kidnap."

*   *   *

It's 4 a.m. as Sergeant Michael "Gibby" Gibson reads the typewritten ransom note left on the card table in Lucas Wilson's house...

```
If you want your son back, $1,000,000 is to be wired into
the account of R.W. Rogers, Cayman National Bank. You will
hear from PJ at 2 pm this afternoon as proof he is alive. You
have until 3 pm bank closing time, to wire us the million.
As soon as it arrives, he will be released. If not, he dies.
Follow these instructions to the letter. Do not depend on the
police to assist you. The fact that we have both your son and
one of their own is proof of their ineptness.
```

Cassie has already read the note several times and is barely hanging on to reality. It's been three hours since she discovered PJ gone and Lucas unconscious. She's been popping Advil and Valium to fight tension migraine and panic. She wonders why so many police personnel and forensic experts are there now, but so few last night. Sergeant Gibson is taking things very hard. He looks as wasted as she feels.

Gibson is beating himself up, *Too many crime scenes following this poor kid around. You have to do better by her. The two man guard you put on the boy just wasn't good enough. One sleeping on the job. The other inside, taken too easily.* Gibby has been turning it over, and it's starting to stink.

Cassie says to him, "I'm gonna pay it. I don't want the damn money anymore. It's meant nothin' but bad luck."

The veteran detective puts an arm around her like she was one of his own daughters, "Darlin', I know I haven't earned your trust. But I will before this is over. Don't give in to them. You don't have to pay anything yet. We've got 'til two o'clock. I'll bring him back."

She tries hard to swallow her fear, "And if you don't? What about his medicine? What if he has an attack? He'll be scared and agitated. That'll bring on the Asthma. He may not even survive 'til 2 p.m. without his pills, let alone an inhaler!"

Gibson is well aware of the medical scenario. It's one way he plans to find PJ. He tells her, "Your son is a very smart kid. I hear he's skipped two school grades already. He's certainly bright enough to let them know if he feels an attack coming on. He'll tell them what he needs. If they want the money, it's in their best interest to take care of him."

Then, he decides to share something possibly encouraging, "Frankly Cassie, my gut and Luke's version of what went down, tells me the Mafia's not involved this time. But a bad cop might be. A million dollars is a big temptation. I think I have a good idea who we're dealing with."

After the harrowing exchange with Cassie, Gibson takes Lucas Wilson aside once again. The old landlord may lack a formal education, but he's smart. His instincts are good and he carries the authority of age. Gibby says, "Let's go over this one more time, Luke."

Lucas is firm in his previous statements, "Like ah said, ah'm sho he put somethin' in mah drink. Ah jes' don't get sleepy as early as midnight." He shakes his head, "And ol' Luke don't lose no five poker hands in a row to the likes a him. Mah eyes wus closed but ah hears him goin' behind me jus' b'fo ah gots hit. It wern't no break-in. No suh, that Mafia dog won't hunt."

Gibby trusts the old man's recollection and instincts. "Luke, I believe you got it right. Lang put his partner out too; he was found sleeping in the squad car. Officer Lang has gone rogue. I got nine hours to find PJ. And a rotten apple cop, too. "

At 5 a.m., he confers with his detectives and sends them back to the station house. They have a lot to do under tight time constraints. Next, he calls to enlist the aid of the OPD Detective Division Commander. Extra staff people are approved. Their task is to alert every hospital, physician and drugstore within a five hundred mile radius of Orlando. The police are to be immediately informed of any Asthma prescriptions.

CHAPTER 24

Fifty-nine year old Detective Sergeant Michael Gibson hasn't slept for more than thirty hours. The closest he came to some rest was last night at 1 a.m., after his midnight communication with Dwayne Lang. He'd just sneaked into bed quietly, trying not to disturb his wife Adrienne, when the bedside phone rang.

Which of course, accomplished what he was trying to avoid. Adrienne sleepily asked, "What now?" After thirty-eight years on the job, she's not surprised by a call to her husband in the middle of the night. But this time, when he tells her Cassie's son has been taken, she groans, "Oh no. If that poor girl didn't have bad luck she'd have none at all."

Her husband's response is angry, "It's that goddam money. 'A gift from heaven' she called it. But it's more like a curse from hell. It was why her boy was taken. I got to move fast. In a kidnapping, the first few hours are vital."

He went from home to Lucas Wilson's house where he read the ransom note, made his promise to Cassie and questioned Lucas again and again. As a result, Dwayne "Sonny" Lang and not the Mafia, became his number one suspect.

It's now 8 a.m. Three hours since Gibson put in motion the police effort to identify and locate hundreds of hospitals, physicians and drugstores. All targeted sources were notified directly or by message to report any Asthma, especially Albuterol, prescriptions to the OPD. The ones not yet open for business are told to call back immediately on receipt of the message.

In addition to the manpower-intense task this involves, Gibby has other moves in mind. For one thing, he tries to locate Dwayne's mother. He knows she now lives in Florida. But when he checks Lang's next of kin file, his mother Elsie's address is not there. He suspects her son has seen to that. Now he must get to Lang's own residence. Dwayne won't be there, but maybe something can be found that will lead to his or PJ's whereabouts. At 8:30 that morning he's on his way to the Holden Heights section of Orlando with a two man search team riding behind him.

On the drive to Lang's house, Gibson can't help thinking how good retirement is going to be. *No more innocent victims like Cassie. Or bad guys like Vince Vega and Harry McIntyre. No more crazy hours and Mafia assholes to deal with. And lots more time with Adrienne, three daughters and seven grandchildren.* Only a month left on the job. Right now he's damn near a burnout. He needs to get off the job and on a pension. Few cops deserve it more.

But first, he has to throw that 300 pound monkey off his back. And see the happy look on Cassie's face when he hands PJ back to her.

He and his men do a thorough ninety minute search of the modest rental in Holden Heights. But without success. Dwayne Lang is good at avoiding discovery. He's been at it for years as both a Cicero gang member and a Chicago cop. He knows how searches are done and what cops look for. But Gibby has been at police detection work for damn near forty years and overlooks nothing, no matter how seemingly insignificant. That's why he spots a piece of scrap paper sticking to the side of an otherwise empty trash container.

Still slightly damp and tomato-stained, it looks like it was torn from what might have been a sales receipt. Turning it over, he can barely read a faded letterhead:

+ ABATE +
Residential Pest Control
227 Marsh Road, St. Cloud, Fl 34773

St. Cloud, in Osceola County, is an hour away. That area includes Alligator Lake and is semi-rural. A company from there wouldn't be doing business in Orlando. *So what's this receipt doing here?* Gibby calls Abate at 11:45 and identifies himself. They verify that their customers are only local. Strictly home owners and condo associations. He asks for a list of customer names. He's told they'll be happy to send one.

He says, "No good. This is an emegency. Right now won't be too soon." He then waits patiently as a girl with a slow rebel accent reads a ten-minute-long lineup of residents they serve. When she gets to the name 'Lang' in Condo 302, Leisure Village, he says, "Okay honey, you can stop right there."

Sergeant Gibson reaches up and puts the magnetized blue flasher on the roof of his Dodge Charger. It'll get him where he's going faster. If he makes good time, it will take an hour. Ten minutes into his trip on Route 4, he gets a voice on his P25 two-way radio, "A call came in to OPD Headquarters five minutes ago. From a Doctor Brookings. He sent in a prescription for Albuterol to a Walgreens drugstore in St. Cloud."

Bingo. Gibby's adrenalin is pumping fast. And a big monkey is starting to slide off his back. *Gotcha. It won't be long now Sonny, you rogue bastard.* He radios back, ordering squad cars to the Leisure Village location. Tells headquarters he'll alert the local sheriff himself. He orders "Sirens off on all cars a mile short of location perimeter. Keep to the perimeter only and avoid being sighted."

Gibson turns off Route 4 onto 244, taking him through Osceola to St. Cloud. He's putting it together, *Lang picking that location makes sense. It's a short trip to Melbourne on the coast, where he can catch a boat to the Cayman Islands. Where the ransom money can't be traced.*

He checks his watch. It's 12:50. He figures his ETA at Leisure Village to be 1:30. Still enough time before the 2 p.m. phone call to Cassie. Unfortunately, he didn't figure on a fatal accident near Alligator Lake that involves a small sedan and a big semi. Lots of flashing ambulance lights and backed-up traffic just ahead.

An hour delay, at least.

CHAPTER 25

It was about 11 a.m. when Gibson found the torn receipt at Lang's house in Holden Heights that was now leading him to the condo in St. Cloud.

At the same time in St. Cloud, PJ opens his eyes and sees nothing familiar. At first, he thinks he's dreaming. Then, climbs out of his cot to look around. There's some juice and cereal set out on a tray. Breakfast for him? He tries the door, but it's bolted from outside.

Elsie Lang doesn't hear him. Her son Dwayne carried the unconscious youngster here early this morning. Their plan is to keep him locked in the windowless den of her condo until two o'clock, when the ransom demand call would be made.

Elsie is neither anemic nor ailing, as her son and a falsified medical document claimed. It got Dwayne their transfer from Chicago to Orlando.

Actually, his mother is an attractive, fifty-six year old woman staying in a small, tired condo that smells of old age. It's part of a complex called Leisure Village. She hates the place but knows she won't be here much longer. Keep the kid for a few more hours. Get the million wired to the Cayman Islands where it can't be traced. Then on to a nice life in the Bahamas. The larcenous mom has participated with her son in many illicit schemes. They are experienced scammers and grifters. But this is the biggest and riskiest deal they've ever done.

Elsie figures, *No big risk, no big reward*. Besides, she has her own backup plan. *You had no idea it was a kidnapping. You were just taking temporary care of a boy your cop son told you he picked up on the street as a runaway.* Throwing her son over to save herself is a definite option.

Betrayal has always been in the family genes.

Meanwhile, PJ realizes he's locked in and starts banging on the door, "Is anybody there? Where am I?" He has a pretty good idea. *It must be those Mafia guys. You've been kidnapped for a ransom. Seen that stuff on TV. These must be the same guys who were after your daddy Tony.*

And now, he knows he's in Tony kind of trouble. Would they kill him if they didn't get their ransom? He bangs louder on the door, finally starts kicking at it. And soon starts to feel tightness in his chest.

He hears Elsie Lang's voice, "Stop making so much noise in there. Every thing is okay, nobody's going to hurt you. Just stay cool."

PJ shouts through the door, "How can I stay cool when I'm bein' kidnapped? Where am I? And who are you?"

"Nonsense honey, you are not being kidnapped. Just kept safe so you can't run away again." That's her story and she's sticking to it.

"What are you sayin'? I never ran away. I went to sleep in Luke's house. Bein' guarded by Officer Lang. That's the last thing I remember. Please let me out of here, m'am." Anxiety is taking it's toll. PJ is getting that old familiar feeling. A tight chest and the "wheezing" has started. He says, "I need my medicine. Do you have it?"

Elsie immediately thinks, *Uh-oh. What the hell is this all about? Dwayne never said anything about needing medicine.* He's in Melbourne right now confirming the boat arrangements for this afternoon. This is a complication she doesn't need. Leaning against the door she says, "What kind of medicine?"

PJ answers through heavy breathing, "I have Asthma. Bad. I need my inhaler and my piscripshun. The name is kinda long, starts with the letter 'A'. It's called 'Albaral', I think. If I don't get it, I won't be able to breathe."

She can now hear the increasing difficulty in his voice. Elsie's getting some tightness in her own chest. She calls Dwayne's cell. No answer.

Leaves a message: "Wherever the fuck you are, you better get back here fast." Then she phones her local family physician, a GP named Albert Brookings. Asks him for a prescription. "My grandson is having an Asthma attack. He needs an inhaler and a drug that sounds like 'Albaral'."

Dr. Brookings corrects her, "It's 'Albuterol'. I'll call in a prescription for you. Meanwhile, go to the drugstore and get your grandson an over-the-counter Singulair Inhaler." By noon, Elsie Lang is in her Honda Civic driving to the local Walgreens drugstore for PJ's inhaler. And still cursing her son. At 12:30, PJ has his inhaler. When Elsie handed it to him, he tried to run past her. But his effort was weak and left him even more winded. The den door is locked again and he's sitting in a chair with his back straight up, like his mom always tells him. The inhaler helps. But his fight for each breath will get increasingly difficult.

Meanwhile, Dwayne has returned. He and Elsie are elsewhere in the condo having a heated argument. He says to her, "Why the fuck did you have to call the fucking doctor? Mike Gibson's no fool. He'll canvas every doc around who prescribes anything for Asthma. Couldn't you just get him a pocket breather?"

Tension is coming off them in waves. She fumes, "I did get him an inhaler. That's why he's still breathing. But it's only a temporary solution. The doctor said he needed the Albuterol. He said any excitement could bring on a deadly attack. Don't you think what happened to him just might amount to excitement? Would you prefer I took him to a hospital? Or let him die?"

Elsie gets right in her son's face, " Without his medicine, how's the kid going to talk to his mother on the phone?" Her tone is seriously sarcastic, "Grifting is one thing. Kidnapping and negligent homicide are slightly more serious. One can only hope you are up to the challenge." Dwayne's shoulders go slack in capitulation, "Okay, get the goddam prescription. But hurry it up. Be back here by 1:30. We gotta get the kid ready for the call."

*   *   *

At 1:15, Gibby is abandoning his car on the shoulder of Route 244.

78

He was going nowhere in the jammed, backed-up traffic and can't afford to wait it out. He grabs his cell phone and takes off running for Leisure Village. He estimates that if he can get there at 1:30 by car, it could take him at least until 2 pm on foot. They'll be on the phone by then. He has to do better.

As he runs, he calls the local sheriff's office and requests a pickup. He's told the only two patrol cars available are behind the accident and can't get through any better than he could. He realizes the squad cars he ordered from headquarters will suffer the same fate. To make matters worse, his cell phone is sputtering, low on batteries and out of any decent range. Detective Sergeant Michael Gibson is now officially on his own.

By 1:45 pm, Florida's heat is peaking. Gibby is drenched in sweat and sucking wind. He starts counting the hours since he's had any sleep. Gets up to forty. Those hours and his nearly sixty years are taking their toll. The body is aching in angry protest. The brain is like a computer on overload, ready to crash.

But he forces mind and feet to keep going, *You've traveled a lot of roads in your life that weren't paved, weren't easy. This is just another hard road. Hang in.*

He now pushes Cassie to the front of the mind line. He pictures her happy face when he puts PJ back into her arms. Yes, he's badly in need of motivation. And younger legs. Only stubborn will power keeps him going. *Run for you life. Better yet, run for PJ's.*

Gibby checks his watch for the umpteenth time at 1:55.

At exactly then, the Valiums are dancing in Cassie's brain. Lots of things in her life have gone wrong, but she's never been so distraught. She waits tearfully on edge, with police tuned in, for her phone to ring.

CHAPTER 26

By 1961, Russell Underwood and Savannah Lindstrom had become a match made in hell.

To an artist, the color black is in reality not a color at all. It's the absence of light. However, various degrees of black can still be detected visually. But *true blackness* cannot be seen. It's in the mind, heart and soul. True blackness occurred when fate brought together a brilliant serial killer with a beautiful murderess.

The extraordinary relationship began that first day in Russell's office. Of course, their steamy affair was risky and light years beyond professional ethics. That never bothered either of them. She thrived on living at the edge and so did he. Besides, Russell was by now well above the law. Simply too clever to get caught.

During their first months together, he taught her the legal process. In turn, Savannah taught Russell as well. She swept him to levels of eroticism he never knew existed. The sex was often perversely violent, befitting their psychotic impulses and instincts.

Meanwhile, her murder trial looms. Russell has been successful in getting a change of venue to Jacksonville. A preliminary hearing has taken place during which the prosecution proves by prima facie case that first degree murder charges are valid. This is followed by a formal arraignment in which Savannah, the defendant, pleads "Not Guilty".

Thirty days later, pre-trial conferences start. Prosecution and defense attorneys meet with the judge and depositions take place. The judge is Leon Haskell, an old timer who has ruled in Russell's favor before.

Enough times in fact, that he's rumored to be in the latter's pocket. Primary prosecutors from the Jacksonville DA's office are District Attorney Carl Branson and Marion Weathers, a veteran trial attorney, and two assistants. Russell and his team from Underwood and Associates represents Savannah.

The case moves to trial phase. Affidavits are signed and witness lists exchanged. Then jury selection takes place. It's a task that suits Russell well. The right jury is vital to any trial and he's damned good at the selection process. But just in case, he has his investigators look into the background of what he anticipates might be any especially difficult jurors. He also prepares meticulously in smaller ways. Such as having one of his paralegals hang around the Circuit Clerk's office on the chance that something pertaining to the case can be useful.

After a lengthy, arduous process, eight women and four men are chosen for the jury panel. Due to the degree of trial notoriety, the District Attorney files a motion to sequester the jury.

The trial starts on an oppressively hot and humid August day in 1962. The location is the Duval County Courthouse, an impressive new building located in downtown Jacksonville. On the day of the trial, East Bay Street, where the courthouse rises majestically, is transformed into something resembling an outdoor Rock Concert. The famous, glamorous model Savannah Lindstrom is on trial for the murder of her wealthy husband. And the furor over her guilt or innocence is not limited to Florida. Every media outlet from coast to coast is covering what has been labeled "The Celebrity Trial of the Decade".

For weeks, prosecution and defense alike are inundated with requests and interviews. Attorneys from both sides appear daily in newspapers and on TV. Russell Underwood for one, luxuriates in the attention. If he wasn't the state's best known trial lawyer before, he is now.

Like so many people all over the state and country, Preston Dylan Jennings, now seventy-two years old and retired, follows events with interest. He knows of a carefully hidden character trait in his ex son-in-law. Curiosity is calling him. Has Russell changed for the better or worse? Of course, he has no way of knowing just how much worse.

Preston wants to watch the trial first-hand and observe a mature Underwood for himself. Betsy and Abbey are curious, too. It becomes a family affair. Five year old Cassie Jean is left in the care of her nanny, Gussie. Preston uses his considerable influence to get "special visitor" passes to the trial and books his wife, his daughter and himself into a nearby hotel suite.

The trial takes place in the most spacious and impressive upper floor courtroom of the Duval County Courthouse. By 8 a.m., every seat in the spectator gallery, including the media section, is occupied. Preston, Betsy and Abbey are seated in the first row bench behind the short rail that separates them from the well of the courtroom. The rectangular table immediately in front of them is occupied by the prosecutors. The table to their left is where Savannah, Russell and his legal team are located.

Russell is immaculately attired in a black suit and striped tie. He's right out of Central Casting... the perfect portrait of a mature, confident, successful attorney. Savannah wears flats, a conservative grey business suit and glasses she doesn't need. Her long, auburn hair is tied back in a bun. It's Russell's attempt to tone-down innate glamour.

Twelve occupants in the Jury Box are stirring nervously. The court stenographer and several bailiffs are in position and ready.

Room clamor hushes and all rise as the Honorable Leon Haskell is announced. Haskell, a stickler for procedure and a true showman, puts things under way with a flourish of his robe and a hammer of his gavel.

"The Celebrity Trial of the Decade" atarts promptly at 9 a.m.

CHAPTER 27

It took a year to get to trial. And to everyone's amazement, it was over in a week. Officially concluded when the jury took less than two hours to reach a verdict. The short length of such a major trial is without precedent in recent legal annals. Russell's team was planning on at least two months.

The shocking brevity can be attributed to the supreme confidence of the prosecution. District Attorney Carl Branson, with a massive backlog of cases, decides to go for the kill quickly. Thus, he will enhance his reputation while also saving tax-payer money. (City expenses connected with the trial have already tripled original estimates and allocations.)

Branson loves the idea of defeating Underwood in record time and is well prepared with a star witness to put on the stand late Thursday, the fourth trial day. He plans a closing argument on Friday. Swift justice.

At the start of the trial, opening statements go smoothly for both prosecution and defense. However, on his way back from the jury box, Russell Underwood gets a jolt. He spots Preston, Betsy and Abbey in the first row of the spectator gallery. It's been many years since his humiliating banishment from Presthaven, but he has no problem identifying them.

Of course, he's now wearing the mask of civility and charm. He gives them a warm smile of recognition. But under the cloak of good will, a dark genius goes immediately to work, *So the flies have come to the spider! At an inconvenient time to kill, perhaps. But still, a worthy challenge. And a unique opportunity to accelerate your plan for revenge. First, the women.*

Now, if Underwood has his way, Preston Jennings will leave

Jacksonville all by himself.

Meanwhile, as Preston watches Russell in action, he cannot help thinking, *If there's a monster under that slick facade, you made a serious mistake not having him prosecuted. For what he did to Abbey, he'd never have gotten a license to practice law.*

The fact that Russell Underwood can juggle both a trial for murder and a *plan* for murder is a testament to genius.

As far as the trial is concerned, based on affidavits and depositions, the prosecution begins to call their witnesses to establish both circumstantial and direct evidence. The defense then cross-examines those witnesses in attempts to challenge their credibility. The first few trial days go routinely and with few surprises. Groundwork is being patiently established by Savannah's counselors for a long-term defense.

But District Attorney Branson will have none of that. He'll play his best card Thursday afternoon. By Friday, the last day of the work week, it should be all but over.

*   *   *

Meanwhile, Russell is conducting his own due diligence both day and night. When in a killing mode, he uses a variety of clever disguises and a collection of hotel passkeys. He now employs them for a nightly reconnoitering of the Crown Plaza Hotel, where it was easy to locate the Jennings family. What he suspected about Preston is confirmed. The Welshman still loves to stay up late, drinking. He's in the "English Pub Room" just off the hotel lobby every night, "chatting-up" his bar mates until 2 a.m. Meanwhile, Betsy and Abbey always go to their rooms directly after dinner, no later than 8 p.m. Russell has already verified room numbers.

By Thursday night, the fourth day of the trial and his third night perusing the Crown Plaza, Russell has solidified his plan. The women's demise will take place Friday about midnight, when Preston will be in the bar drinking and socializing.

Underwood savors the thought of Jennings returning to his beloved Presthaven, bereft, alone and left with only his money for comfort. But that won't last, either. It may take a few years, but he'll get the fortune, too. That's where Savannah comes in.

After she's acquitted, of course. Tomorrow, as a highly skilled lawyer, he will ambush District Attorney Carl Branson's star witness. In the evening, he'll serve as both judge and jury in the execution of the Jennings women.

CHAPTER 28

District Attorney Carl Branson deals his "ace" to the court on Thursday afternoon immediately following the luncheon recess. He calls to the stand Carmen Robles.

The Underwood team has placed Robles well down on their list of prosecution witnesses. Her move up the list comes as a surprise and is an indication that Brandon is after a fast kayo. That's fine with Russell since he's well prepared with a deadly counter punch for whenever she makes her appearance.

A combination of depositions, affidavits, inside information from Savannah and a visit to the crime scene has given him all he needs. The rest is up to his skill as a cross examiner.

Carmen Robles, like Savannah Lindstrom, has been "down-dressed" for the occasion. But not as successfully. Her hair is too obviously dyed blonde, her flowered dress is slightly too clingy and her three inch heels should have been flats. Russell regards this as shoddy preparation on the prosecution's part, no matter how confident Branson is in his rush to judgement. Carmen has the natural coloring of a Latina but also the bronzed skin of a serious Florida sun worshipper. Magenta lips glow within an attractive, sharp-featured face. In briefing his defense team, Russell has described Carmen as a rather "hot tamale". He knows it's the prosecution's mistake not to more drastically lower her temperature.

The D.A. establishes that Ms. Robles has been a maid in the employ of Mr. and Mrs. Benjamin Murcer for nearly two years and is familiar with the goings on between husband and wife. Savannah is made out to be a gold-digging bitch with no affection for her husband other than his money. They constantly argued over her frivolous spending and she was totally indifferent to him. This of course, is consistent with testimony by other prosecution witnesses.

Branson, cutting to the chase, asks Carmen, "Ms. Robles, tell us about the day of the murder..."

He gets no further. Russell is on his feet with a loud "Objection".

Judge Haskell immediately says, "Sustained". Then admonishes the esteemed D.A., "You know better, Mr. Branson. Don't make that mistake again."

Branson corrects himself on the use of a no-no word, "On the day of Mr. Murcer's *demise*, precisely how did you witness the events?"

Carmen Robles has been well rehearsed. Under Branson's relentless interrogation, she proceeds with a detailed description of how Savannah shot and killed her husband. How her voice was heard shouting "Die, you bastard". And then the shot. And finally the actual sight of Mrs. Murcer at the top of the stairs, still aiming the gun at her fallen husband, who was on his knees trying to hold his exploding stomach together.

It is an effective testimony. The jury is obviously acknowledging the information revealed by a formidable witness for the prosecution. The D.A. has expertly led Carmen to where he wanted to go. If he was able to make his closing statement right now, there would be little doubt about the verdict. Carl Branson, full of confidence, pauses for a full thirty seconds. It's a lawyer's ploy to allow a testimony to hang in the air before moving on. He then makes a sweeping arm gesture and says to Russell, "Your witness."

But a cross examination won't take place now, and he knows it. Branson has used up the entire afternoon, leaving the jury with exactly the lingering impression of guilt he was after.

His Honor Leon Haskell adjourns court for the day and instructs the jury not to discuss the case. Cross proceedings will start promptly at 9 a.m. tomorrow.

CHAPTER 29

On Friday at 9 a. m., court bailiffs and the defense have set up a large easel that holds an impressive four by six foot poster board, easily visible to the jury box and the witness stand.

It displays a detailed ground floor plan of the Murcer's impressive residence. The locations of the shooter and the victim are marked with large X's. The plan shows a massive twenty square foot entrance lobby off the front door. It separates the bedroom wing on the right from a utility wing on the left that includes the kitchen, pantry, side door and maid's bedroom.

Carmen Robles is back on the witness stand as Russell Underwood approaches both her and the jury. He explains how important it is for "all of us" to understand every physical detail of the scenario in which Ben Murcer was shot to death.

In addressing the witness, Russell is careful to use a non-confrontational tone. Jurors do not like lawyers attacking and badgering witnesses, especially women. He's already observed this in their reaction to the D.A.'s own attack method. His considerable trial experience has taught him that in order to be won over, a jury must be wooed slowly... with logic, emotion and trust.

It wasn't easy for Russell to repress his sociopathic impulses towards women. In assuming a courteous and gentlemanly manner, he must do an acting job worthy of an Academy Award. His tone is restrained, deferential, "As you know, Ms. Robles, Savannah Murcer has never denied the shooting. But the lobby was dark and quite some distance from where she stood at the top of that staircase. In a frightened state, at a very early hour of the morning, she thought she was protecting herself from an intruder or a burglar. Not a husband." He asks, "Didn't you say you heard Mrs. Murcer yell out before the shot was fired?"

Carmen's response comes quickly, "Yes. She said 'Die, you bastard'."

Russell then asks her to show the jury precisely where she was when she heard that said, and when she saw Savannah with her weapon at the top of the staircase. The witness points to a place at the far end of the lobby where her bedroom is located. He then leads her and the jury through a series of polite questions that establish where and how she sleeps, as well as the dimensions and distances on the entire first floor display.

He is able to do this because he and his team had explored the Murcer residence quite thoroughly. With the door to the maid's bedroom closed, only a gunshot, not a voice, could be heard over the forty foot distance from the top of the staircase to inside Carmen's room. He says, "Since you've already said you sleep with your bedroom door closed, the only way you could hear Mrs. Murcer's voice is because the door was at least partially open. Is that correct?"

A good lawyer knows the answer before he asks the question. When she answers in the affirmative, it's time to spring the trap."Ms. Robles, you do realize you are under oath? This is not just a deposition. You have sworn on a bible in a court of law. The penalty for perjury will send you to prison for a long time."

If Carmen's face wasn't already the color of copper, it would have turned pale. Before she can respond, Carl Branson leaps to his feet with a loud objection. He says Russell is intimidating and threatening his witness. Judge Haskell overrules the objection, "There is nothing wrong with a lawyer reminding a witness she is under oath".

It's time now to follow awe with shock. Russell's tone is still understated as he says, "Do you always leave your private bedroom door open at night? Or just when you want to signal others, including Mr. Murcer, when they arrive late... that you are available?"

The disturbance in the courtroom moves from palpable to loud. Judge Haskell pounds his gavel and calls for quiet. The prosecution's star witness is quickly breaking down under each politely and evenly asked question. Another masterful Underwood performance is taking place. Carmen eventually must admit to "entertaining" men on the premises and to the fact that Savannah may have mistaken her husband for one of them.

Russell's demeanor remains calm as he leads Carmen through a series of admissions... that she knew first hand of Ben Murcer's infidelity, but had no such knowledge of Savannah's. That she was getting paid for sex by Ben Murcer and others, and had effectively turned the Murcer home into "a cat house". That she had an innately jealous bias towards her lover's glamorous wife. Finally, that her own veracity as a witness has now been rendered unacceptable.

Russell says, "I don't doubt you heard Mrs. Murcer say "Die, you bastard". Nor has she ever denied it." His voice is still reasonable when he asks, "But isn't it possible she would say that very same thing to someone who was not her husband, but instead a dangerous intruder?"

Her answer must be and is, a contrite and simple "yes".

After such a debacle, Branson tries desperately to recoup with his redirect, but he fears too much damage has been done. He curses himself for not vetting Carmen Robles more carefully. For his zeal to win big in a high profile trial. And for an aggressive rush to judgement. The jury's verdict will be fast, alright. But probably not the one he anticipated.

D.A. Carl Brandon feels in his gut that he's not met his burden of proof. The prosecution rests, hoping for a miracle. Closing statements are made. Russell respectfully asks the jurors to perform their legal and moral duty and vote "Not Guilty" if they have any doubt whatsoever.

It takes less than two hours for them to reach agreement and return with a verdict.

CHAPTER **30**

District Attorney Branson knows it may not be good news when the jurors complete their deliberations so quickly.

Told the jury is ready with a verdict, members of the press from A.P., U.P., and all TV broadcast outlets rush back, along with an overflow crowd of spectators. Betsy, Abbey and Preston are among the gallery as they slide into their front row seats. Noise settles down and the ambiance becomes one of hushed expectation as the jury moves into the courtroom.

While Russell was certain Savannah would have performed well, he avoided putting her on the stand in her own defense. No need. In his mind, the trial had already been won with his destruction of the D.A.'s chief witness. Absolutely confident of a fast outcome, he and Savannah remained in the courtroom while others left. They whispered about the exciting and deadly events that are going to take place this evening at the Crown Plaza Hotel.

Two rows and all twelve seats of the jury box are now occupied. Jurors and spectators await another flourished entrance from Judge Leon Haskell. He is quite disappointed that the trial has concluded so quickly. There are only minutes left to bask in national notoriety. He enters, taps his gavel and, in his most authoratative voice says, "The court will come to order."

He then goes through the formality of asking the jury forewoman if a verdict has been reached. A pretty, high school math teacher named Roseann Foglio says, "Yes Your Honor, we have reached a verdict."

He asks, "How say you?"

"By unanimous vote, we find the defendant... Not Guilty."

The courtroom erupts at the pronouncement. There are several raps of Haskell's gavel to restore order. He thanks the jury, but before he's able to officially close proceedings, the press is stampeding out. Cell phones and cameras have not been permitted in court, so reporters rush madly to call-in and file their stories. Savannah hugs Russell and thanks the others in his firm who have participated in her defense. Underwood looks over Savannah's shoulder and catches Preston's eye in the front row.

Preston locks into a look that comes from the shining star of Florida's legal world. Russell is smiling once more. But this time it's a frigid smile... one that involves the mouth but leaves the rest of the face behind. At that moment, the old tycoon feels an inward chill. He now has the answer to a question he's wrestled with. Has his ex-son-in-law changed? Indeed he has. *For the worse*.

*   *   *

The asphalt cuts through cabbage palms and scrubby pines like a black scar in the landscape. Hypnotic waves of heat are coming off the road ahead. Gibbey's eyes are burning inside a sweat-soaked face. His feet are lead weights that have to be lugged along with the rest of him. From a slow trot to a limping walk, his tortured body somehow still pushes forward.

He's on the edge of collapse and capitulation when he sees it. Is it real, or is it a mirage he's looking at through those shimmering heat waves? Was God teasing? Or answering prayers?

The low-level roadside sign is about forty yards ahead. Bright orange script letters that gradually come into focus... *"Leisure Village"*. The exhausted cop looks at his watch yet again. 2 p.m.

At that moment, Dwayne "Sonny" Lang has PJ in the crook of his arm and is dialing Cassie's number.

Meanwhile, Gibson stumbles through the retirement community entrance and searches frantically for the Lang condo. *Where in hell is unit 302? There it is, Palm Lane, two villas ahead.* He arrives at his destination on unsteady legs, struggling to keep his balance and his wits as he circles around to a side window.

They are sitting at a table in the kitchen. He can see PJ, with tears streaming down his eight year old, trying-to-be-brave face. His shoulders are shaking, his chest is heaving. Dwayne and Elsie Lang are sitting to either side. It's five minutes past two o'clock. The call to Cassie has been made.

Gibby thinks, *Still time for a quick call back. But you have to move fast.* He unholsters his service revolver and rushes to the side door.

In his haste, and from his angle on the tableau viewed through the window, he fails to see something important. It's the Beretta at Sonny Lang's back, tucked into his waistband.

CHAPTER 31

Gibby points his Smith & Wesson at the side door lock and blows it away. Throwing the door open with a force that shatters glass, he moves quickly inside. Dwayne and Elsie Lang are frozen in shock.

As he holds his weapon on them, he motions PJ to his side, telling him, "Have a seat buddy, stay calm and collect your breath. Every thing's gonna to be okay now." He says to the Langs, "Hands behind your heads, both of you." Then he gives PJ a consoling pat on the head and says, "I'm sure you know your phone number. Betcha your mom will be glad to hear back from you so soon."

PJ grabs the phone and excitedly tells his joyful mom what just happened. About to leave for her bank, there is now no need to wire one million dollars to an account in the Caymans. But far more importantly than any amount of money, Cassie has her son back. When Gibby takes the phone, she thanks him profusely through tears of gratitude.

"You kept your promise. I'll be forever grateful. How can I possibly thank you enough?"

"The look on your face when I hand PJ over will be all the thanks I need, sweetheart." He hangs up and immediately dials headquarters to locate his backup. Still winded and shaky as he does so, he takes his eyes off Sonny for a few seconds. It's what Lang has been waiting for. With a left hand still placed behind his head, he slowly lowers his right, to the back of his waist. With Gibson's eyes momentarily diverted, the kidnapper whips the Beretta out from behind his back.

Gibby's peripheral vision catches the sudden movement. Although he's on the verge of heat exhaustion, fortunately his own weapon is still in hand. The body is spent, but reflexes respond with a pull of the trigger. His bullet enters Lang's forehead just above and between the eyes.

Elsie Lang screams and reaches over the table to her mortally wounded son. Gibson says, "Sit back, Mrs. Lang and leave that gun exactly where it is on the floor. You don't want to be going where your son is right now. It's even hotter down there."

PJ's eyes are wide with the wonder of what just transpired... the most exciting thing he'll ever witness in his entire life. It doesn't help his breathing any, but the good guy shot the bad guy. Right now, that's all that matters. The phone line is still open and a police dispatcher's voice on the other end asks, "Gibby, what's with the gunfire? Are you okay? What the fuck's goin' on?"

The veteran detective's response is slow and considered, "Just took out a bad cop. Self-defense. Righteous kill." He adds, "Get my guys here ASAP with a medic for treating Asthma. And send a meat wagon. I got somebody needs transportation to the morgue."

Backup squad cars and an ambulance have finally gotten through the tie-up on Route 244. All the noise brings out many curious, elderly Leisure Village inhabitants. They watch as Elsie Lang is escorted from her condo in handcuffs and her son is carried out in a body bag.

Meanwhile, PJ is being treated by medics and breathing better. Gibby sits on a sidewalk curb, chatting with his congratulating peers. He downs three Cokes and four Almond Joys, thirst quenchers and energizers to keep him going. He has one last chore before some badly needed shuteye.

It's a duty he wouldn't miss for the world. By 6 p.m., he's handing PJ back to Cassie. There have never been three happier people. Detective Sergeant Gibson is now ready for a peaceful retirement.

Retirement, yes. Peaceful, no.

CHAPTER 32

Savannah Lindstrom, with the help of Russell Underwood, has literally gotten away with murder. Outsmarting the law is an incredible turn-on. But the celebratory sex will have to wait.

First, surrounded by security, they must wade through crowds of spectators both inside the courtroom and out. They blink their way past hundreds of camera flashes. Relentless questions from the local, national and international press. Then interviews for television.

Hours later, they're finally alone. Sitting in Russell's rented penthouse, they open a bottle of Dom Perignon and click crystal in self-congratulation. They watch TV and narcissistically critique each other's performance. Cunning plus celebrity plus champagne equals erotic arousal. What happens next can't accurately be described as making love. Consensual, mutual rape would be more apt. They move violently from room to room. Two deviant minds and strong bodies are in sync... each seeking sexual gratification through painful pleasure.

For his entire life, Russell had been so full of himself that there was no room for anyone else. Now, with soul mate Savannah, he's even more formidable. And deadly.

But their victorious day has only just begun. Colossal egos, along with motives of wealth and revenge are still to be satisfied. The long range plan is, of course, to relieve Preston Jennings of the fortune they will subsequently share. That scheme begins tonight with the elimination of the wealthy patriarch's wife and daughter.

First, Russell's once mother-in-law must be terminated. And quickly, allowing time for the more lingering and painful death of his ex-wife. Russell thinks about Abbey. She's still an attractive woman in her mid forties. Now with a child and so much to look forward to. But a woman who shunned him, making no effort to reconcile. She'll pay dearly for that with a brutal rape. He'll enjoy looking into eyes filled with panic and regret as his hands tighten around her throat.

Underwood had always kept himself well informed about the Jennings family. He knew of Abbey's marriage to war hero Jon Dornwell. And after his death in Vietnam, the birth of their child. He's determined to make an orphan of that girl. True revenge has no limits. Nor does a true psychopath.

Tonight, Russell and Savannah will be in disguise. Her task is to keep Preston in sight, make sure he doesn't leave the hotel pub while Russell is dealing with the women. She'll phone from the lobby to set the executions in motion.

*   *   *

At 11 p.m., the Crown Plaza is teeming with guests. It's Friday evening, the start of a busy weekend in Jacksonville. Many of the visitors were attendees of "The Celebrity Trial of the Decade". But none would be able to identify the blonde, bearded cowboy in the Stetson hat and Dingo boots. Nor would they recognize the tall Islamic woman in the loosely wrapped Burqa that covered a sensuous body and the veil that hid a beautiful face.

Savannah is stationed in her Muslim garb at the entrance to the English Pub Room just off the lobby. From there, she is close to a house phone. At 11:30, she calls room 902 where Russell is registered as Bradford Lawrence from Austin, Texas.

She tells him, "He's at the bar drinking and chatting it up. The old fucker's throwing down the second drink of what looks to be at least a five Cutty Sark story."

Underwood does enjoy Savannah's sardonic sense of humor. Now, with supreme confidence, he takes an elevator up to Betsy's floor. Earlier, he'd hooked a "Do Not Disturb" sign on her door handle. Everything is set. If he's seen and remembered in the vicinity, it will be as a blonde, bearded cowboy.

In room 1151, Betsy has ritually fallen asleep while watching television. Russell enters silently with a housekeeper's pass key. He knows the door will be unbolted, waiting for her husband's arrival. Enough light to work by... his victim's face and the sheet she sleeps under are bathed in a pale blue light cast by the TV. He now must move quickly and quietly, without disturbing Abbey in the adjoining room.

He picks up an extra pillow from the king-size bed and whispers, *Life's a bitch, Mrs. Jennings... and then you die.*

The pillow is pushed over a peaceful face with full force. Suddenly, fear is a knife that penetrates Betsy's consciousness. Arms and legs flail out. But an internal light is rapidly leaving her. And hope, as well. Within minutes, the life of a cherished wife and mother is extinguished.

Russell regrets that his former mother-in-law's death was of necessity, relatively merciful. But Abigail won't be so lucky. Police will find her a badly beaten and raped murder victim of the same anonymous intruder.

He quietly keys open the interior connecting door to Abbey's room and moves silently inside. What he finds unnerves him.

CHAPTER **33**

What Russell finds is, in a word, *nothing*. The room is empty without any evidence of Abigail. No luggage. No clothes. No toiletries. No *nothing*.

What he never anticipated was a last minute change of Abbey's plans. She left that afternoon soon after the trial. It was a call from Presthaven that saved her life. Nana Gussie put five year old Cassie Jean on the phone.

Cassie was in tears, "Momma, I miss you. Please come home."

Abbey's heart melted, "I miss you too, baby. I'll start packing right now. See you real soon."

The trial was over anyway, having ended so unexpectedly earlier that afternoon. It had already served the purpose of confirming her previous experience with a despicable man. When the verdict came in, Russell's look of angry triumph and egotistical conceit said it all.

So, after her brief, emotional exchange with Cassie, she made a life-saving decision to go home. Preston and Betsy would check her out of the hotel along with themselves, on Saturday. She left Jacksonville on Friday afternoon in a limo to Presthaven.

*   *   *

When Preston returned to his room at 2 a.m. Saturday morning, he was very drunk. Shedding only shoes and trousers, he fell into bed. When he awakened eight hours later and found his wife still beside him and so strangely quiet, he knew something was terribly wrong.

The aftermath was easily the worst period in his extraordinarily eventful life. A police investigation ensued. Forensics determined that Betsy was suffocated with her pillow. The only good suspect was someone who checked in and out of the Crown Plaza as Brad Lawrence. He was described by the desk clerk and a bellman as a blonde, bearded cowboy. A follow-up investigation found that his identification was bogus. No such person existed. Once again, the police had failed in dealing with a secret serial killer named Russell Underwood.

Preston posted a record reward for information leading to the capture of his wife's killer. But to no avail. Now, in 1962 at age seventy-two, he'd trade everything he'd ever achieved to bring back his beloved Betsy.

Since that wasn't possible, he had staged a funeral worthy of a head of state. Preston mourned for months. As did Abbey. After the death of her husband Jon Dornwell, the loss of her mother sent her into depression.

Despite the most important loss of his life, the stalwart patriarch was not a man to stay down for the count. There were two people left in his family to care for. Having already accumulated all the wealth he'd ever need, he decided to retire and devote his remaining time to a daughter and a grandchild.

Preston Dylan Jennings now lived only for Abigail and her "miracle baby". They'd be lavished with love, attention and just about anything they desired. Cassie would be educated at home. Formally tutored in traditional school curriculums by her granddaddy. Taught also with the wisdom he'd harvested in a lifetime of extraordinary achievement.

Unfortunately, Cassie's fairy tale childhood in Presthaven would end by age ten.

Russell Underwood and Savannah Lindstrom would see to that.

CHAPTER 34

Detective Sergeant Michael Gibson retired in June, 1983. But with the permission of his chief, he still had an important carryover duty to complete.

It took a while to resolve a new strategy for guarding Cassie and PJ. Departmental resources could no longer provide two-man, around the clock protection. Since the kidnap attempt, there were no more threats. But the Mafia, and God knows who else, were still laying low somewhere out there and would not forget about her money.

Gibson's solution was to put Cassie and PJ into something akin to a witness protection plan. It would require changes of appearance, identity and location.

Cassie and trusted friend Manny Delgado, were with Gibby in his office at OPD to discuss the strategy. PJ was home with Lucas Wilson. The most difficult part of the plan would be leaving Luke. Being too old and too grounded in a home in which he'd lived his entire life, he couldn't go with them. But he'd been part of her little family for years and Cassie was reluctant to leave him.

Gibson says, "PJ and you have stayed too long already. They'll catch up with you here. You need to get safely away. Start over. Enjoy your windfall. Leave all the bad stuff behind."

"Right. And leave all my friends behind, too. Like Luke. Like you guys. Like all the girls at the Booby Trap. And all PJ's pals at school." Cassie shrugs sadly, "It seems like I've been runnin' all my life."

Manny refuses to accept any negativity, "Don't worry about the friends baby. You'll make plenty of new and better ones. PJ will, too." Her ex-boss follows a positive declaration with a reassuring smile, "You're going to a great part of the state. And if you stick with Gibby's plan, you won't have to worry who's gonna be around the corner."

The plan is for blonde Cassie Jean Dornwell to become brunette Elizabeth (Liz) Harrison. Gibson has taken care of her new ID. The relocation will be to Southwest Florida. Her bank account has been top-security wired from the First Federal of Orlando to a Bank of America savings account in Ft. Myers. She will live in Bonita Springs, a location near Sanibel Island and Naples. It is her choice of those two high-end places to work. Manny has arranged a restaurant position in either locale for Cassie, alias Liz. She'll be a hostess and front-of-the-house manager. No more bartender/stripper jobs for his favorite underage employee.

As they leave their little garage apartment and climb down those steep stairs for the last time, she thinks, *I'll even miss my "exercise steps".*

But she knew Gibby and Manny were right. She'd never feel secure here again. Not after PJ's kidnapping. That was as hellish as anything she's ever been through.

Cassie muses, *No more hellish, please. Give me some heaven in Southwest Florida.*

CHAPTER 35

Midnight, July 30th 1983. Cassie is heading south on I-75 in her old faithful VW Beetle. Nine year old PJ fits perfectly in her rear view mirror, curled up and sleeping in the back seat. Occasionally, overhead highway lights pick up a glint of silver on his neck. Ever since he's been rescued by Gibby, Cassie makes sure her son is never without Tony's St. Christopher medal.

She now knows there's something else that has to go in the rear view mirror... her previous life.

Gibson and one of his detectives escort them in an unmarked police car. They take turns driving behind and ahead of the VW. After several diversions including one back-track, Gibby's sure they aren't being followed.

Four hours from Orlando, they exit I-75 on Bonita Beach Road. Ten minutes later they're parked in front of Cassie's and PJ's new home.

There is another tearful farewell. As he hugs them, Gibby whispers to Cassie, "I'm officially retired, sweetheart. Turned in the shield." He pats his hip, "But I get to keep Misters Smith & Wesson. So remember, in case you ever need me, I still got my .38 and you still got my number."

*   *   *

Cassie and PJ awaken in morning sunshine to a pleasant surprise. Their new abode is situated on golf course grounds. It's hardly a "Members Only" club. Instead, a short yardage public course called "The Bonita Fairways". But the modest two bedroom condo and the surrounding community are definite improvements on the cramped garage apartment and the old, compressed neighborhood in suburban Orlando.

And it's conveniently located a mile from a strategic thoroughfare, Route 41. From there, it's a two hour drive to Sarasota. That's where, on a corner of the same Route 41 (first called Tamiami Trail), her granddaddy once pumped gas. It was Preston Jennings' first job in 1910, and the very beginning of his phenomenal rise to riches.

The night before she left Orlando, Cassie dyed her blonde hair to a deep brunette, thus accomplishing what she hoped for, a dramatic change in appearance.

PJ was startled, "Is that really you, mom? Wow, you look so different."

"That's the whole idea honey. I'm still your same ol' momma. But now my name is Liz. Our last name is Harrison and we have a whole new life that's gonna be better."

She wanted very much to believe that last part.

It's a hot and humid day, so as soon as Cassie and PJ are settled into their new digs, they venture to Sanibel Island for some cooling Gulf breezes. That's also where they can visit one of the two restaurants Manny has recommended for a new job.

What was not to like about Sanibel? Tropical blooms everywhere. A beautiful beach of white sand with a shoreline that offers up an abundance of great shells for PJ's collection. There are diving Pelicans and leaping Porpoises. Conspicuous Egrets and rare Eagles. With their flip-flops in hand, mother and son wade along water's edge. Afterwards, they visit the restaurant. It's called "The Succulent Prawn", an exclusive, striped awning cafe with a limited number of tables. But it won't be her first choice. She prefers something bigger, offering more tip opportunity. Moreover, her budget will be affected by daily trips across a pricey toll bridge connecting to the mainland. She likes Sanibel, but has money concerns about working there.

Cassie is determined not to dip into her recent fortune. While tempted to do so, she will stay on a budget that befits her restaurant earnings. She's still ambivalent about the money. Is it a blessing or a curse? So she disciplines herself to keep it right where it is, in the bank. It will be used only for medical treatments, as PJ may require them.

Meanwhile, she'll wait for the source of her million dollars to return. Someday, when Tony Roselli comes back to her, they'll spend it together.

For the most part, life has put Cassie in a corner, and she's always had to fight her way out. Her first nine years in Presthaven and the brief marriage to Tony were her only truly happy days. Now, she isn't even sure of her own name. She wonders if it's Dornwell. Or Roselli. Or Harrison. Is it Cassie or Liz?

But one thing's for sure. If PJ and she are to stay safe, she must follow Gibby's edict. It had better be Liz Harrison.

*   *   *

When they changed her name and sent her here, Michael Gibson and Manny Delgado were aware of something Cassie could not know. They had a secret, ulterior motive for dispatching her to Southwest Florida.

When Delgado took Gibson into his confidence, the detective had to make a difficult choice. Would he defy police procedure and put reputation, retirement and pension at risk? Or would he say nothing about what he now knew?

He decided the risk was worth the reward.

Manny knew Cassie well and was sure her choice of work would not be the tiny cafe in Sanibel. She would find the large, beautiful restaurant in downtown Naples much more to her liking and her needs.

And that would serve his and Gibby's scheme very well.

CHAPTER 36

For Cassie and PJ, downtown Naples was love at first sight. In 1983, the pretty little village was still a well-kept secret from the rest of the world. But it soon would become a favored vacation destination, offering near perfect weather throughout the winter, scenic beaches and a relaxed, upscale ambience. Naples became the choice of many wealthy northerners who preferred it's peaceful Gulf location to the traffic on I-95 and the crowded environs of Miami and Palm Beach, on the other side of Alligator Alley.

Cassie's practiced bartender eyes are taking in everything and everyone. The population is skewed towards retirement age. More "snowbirds" than full timers. Well-heeled and well-dressed. Lots of good looking, good tippers. She smiles inwardly, *Plenty of face lifts and tummy tucks. Bet plastic surgeons make a great living here.*

Distinguished looking men in their sixties and seventies are with well-kept women in their thirties and forties. Yes, there is also the "early bird", two-drinks-for-one crowd. But definitely not the Sweet 'N Low packet snatchers you get in less affluent locales.

On Third Street South, she's never seen so many Rolls Royces and Bentleys in one place. Immaculately clean streets everywhere, with blazing florals in oversized sidewalk planters and baskets that hang from ornate lampposts. Charming high-end boutiques named "The Gazebo" and "The Pear Tree" to go along with even loftier names like Cartier and Swarovski.

No way could a service person like her live in a place like this. She and the rest would have at least a thirty minute commute from home.

The restaurant Cassie sought was located on swanky Fifth Avenue. Beautifully designed with wide Tuscan arches, an atrium fountain, stylish, comfortable furniture and Florentine flourishes everywhere. The name was carved in classic Roman letters over tall, cathedral-like Mahogany doors. It read: "DolceAmore".

Italian translation: "Sweet Love". Cassie couldn't help thinking, *I once knew a romantic ladies' man who'd really like that name.*

She will go to the back office and introduce herself to the owner of DolceAmore as the Liz Harrison sent here by Manny Delgado. But first, Cassie decides to have lunch with PJ. She'll look at a menu and get a better feel for the place and for the service. A young hostess seats them at a quiet corner table. It's a task that, along with House Manager, will soon be hers. When she opens the large, leather-bound menu, her pulse suddenly races.

Inside, no listing of cocktails, appetizers or entrees. Just a single sheet of parchment paper.

On it, written in a familiar scrawl, is a single word... *"Mariposa"*.

CHAPTER 37

When the sadness is on him like a blanket, he's always able to throw it off. But remembrances linger.

Roosters crow in Presthaven every morning at 5 a.m. A sliver of light in the east signals dawn. Preston doesn't watch the sunrise because something else catches his mind's eye.

Laying in bed, he time-travels seventy years into his Welsh past. He is three years old. He's running. Little legs are not yet working all that well. He falls hard on a dirt road near the small, thatched-roof cottage where he lives. Loose gravel tears flesh from his calf and knee. There's blood and there's tears. Betsy Hannigan, age five, who lives a few small dwellings away, comes seemingly out of nowhere. She cleanses and bandages his wounds.

Somehow, she was always there. At age seven, when he lost his five year old sister to tuberculosis. Later, when his mum and baby brother died in childbirth. Then, when his pa finally stopped breathing after years of fighting lung disease. Betsy would pray with him, hold his hand and offer comfort.

No stopping the old memories. When he worked at age ten as the town's "dungboy" and was harassed by the foul-mouthed neighborhood lads. It was Betsy who scattered them with some stevedore language of her own.

And it was Betsy who stole the library key that led him to a discovery of America.

Now he recalls an unforgettable night. A passageway to their future. He is in the moldy old Aberdare Library studying English Grammar, learning about nouns and modifiers, verbs and adverbs. At 1 a.m., there is a knock on the back door. It's Betsy, flushed and needy. Something deep inside told her to come to him that night. After many passionate kisses, they clear off a large wooden table back by the stacks. They have sex on that table. For the first time, it is unprotected sex. When reminiscing about that night, they always shared an inside joke that never failed to make them smile. They were surrounded by books at the moment of her conception. That's why Abbey was always such a good reader!

Preston remembers a fight at the mine soon after. As a result, he was fired from his job. Lateness prompted it. His routine was to go to the mine from the library via his flat, where he'd take a catnap and a shower. But at times he studied too long. Sleepless, he'd go directly to the mine. On late arrivals, his foreman would wait in ambush to give him a royal chewing-out.

That foreman, a big, tough veteran named Jack Jacobson had a history of trouble with Preston's father, Dylan. In those days he and Dylan were rivals for the foreman's job. They were known to indulge in fisticuffs on many occasions, especially after hours when they'd downed a few whiskeys at the local pub.

When Preston arrived late for the third time in a month, Jacobson immediately got in his face, "Yer a lazy fookin' bahstad. One more time and yer arse is fired."

Knowing he deserved the verbal assault, Preston said quietly, "Sorry boss. I'll do better."

Encouraged by an unusually submissive response, Jacobson gave him a hard shove and said, "Yer just like yer shiftless dead father, you ain't worth a shite."

Preston now remembers the short fuse he had in those days. Even shorter than later in life. Nobody dishonored his father that way. He hauled off with a right uppercut that broke the bully foreman's nose and put him on his back in a pile of coal. That did it for his job. But it was about time to leave for America anyway.

By then, Preston knew the U.S. map by heart. Florida always intrigued him. Of all the 48 states, it was the only peninsula, jutting out into the Atlantic Ocean and the Gulf of Mexico. And it was warm in winter. A welcome change from the cold, damp chill of his native land. He studied it's history, too. St. Augustine was America's oldest city. Settled half a century before the English landed in Jamestown. Discovered by Ponce de Leon in 1513. The Spanish explorer named it "Florida" for the colorful flora and fauna so abundant there.

Preston recalls his journey south from Ellis Island and the rapid accumulation of wealth in his new land of opportunity. He remembers the idea that came to him early one morning in a little Sarasota diner called "Elsie's Dry Dock". An idea that led to The Gulf Oil Company Storage and Distribution Center that made him a billionaire.

That in turn, enabled him to build his magnificent plantation-like estate in Apopka. It was an accomplishment that once inspired an authoress friend of Betsy's. Margaret Mitchell was so impressed with Presthaven, she renamed it "Tara" for her hugely successful new novel, "Gone With The Wind".

The years have now passed like an epic tale and he's proud of his achievements. But Preston would trade it all for Betsy to be here in bed, beside him. It has been three long years since he so cruelly lost her to an unknown intruder.

His only family now was a daughter and a granddaughter. Abigail still suffers from, and is treated for, depression. But daughter Cassie has become a happy, vibrant and curious child, anxious to learn from her granddaddy. Preston loves, and lives, to teach her.

Meanwhile, he's approaching his mid seventies. But it doesn't mean he's lost his virility. He still has the sex drive, but hasn't had a woman since Betsy. He's now lonely and vulnerable.

A fact that would not escape Russell Underwood and Savannah Lindstrom.

CHAPTER 38

Since the "The Celebrity Trial of the Decade", Russell Underwood's law practice has been booming bigger than ever. He is now a nationally renowned attorney. As years go by, more and more of his time is spent on increasingly important defense cases.

But his alter ego, the unknown serial killer of Betsy Jennings and eleven others, has grown restless. And so has his partner. Savannah Lindstrom wants those Jennings millions and is impatient to proceed with their plan.

Several years have passed since Betsy's murder. Far too long for Savannah to wait for her seduction of Preston. And seduce him she will. The beautiful model and would-be actress is supremely confident of her persuasive powers. Men's brains are below their belts, aren't they? She feels the location of a man's grey matter makes him easy prey. Even her brilliant associate has fallen victim to her charms.

Russell needs Savannah to seduce and help him eliminate Preston. Savannah needs Russell to manipulate and reconstruct his will. Perfect partners in crime. She's more than ready.

But Underwood has insisted on waiting for an ideal opportunity. He's used the precious time away from his busy practice to carefully prepare. With usual cunning, he has hired a private investigator named David Richards, who was formerly Security Chief for a chain of Walmark Super Stores in Tallahassee. Richards is now a thorough and trusted investigator on Russell's personal payroll. His assignment is to tightly monitor Preston Jennings and family.

Dave Richards was an intelligent professional. The first thing he did was perfectly position himself for close observation. After Betsy's murder he went to Preston and convinced him of the need for tighter protection at Presthaven. Richards presented his Walmark Security credentials and was hired. He then had new electronic gates installed and took on some retired cops to patrol and secure the premises on a twenty-four hour watch. It was a smart move in more ways than one. Since he now had two bosses, he also had two salaries.

Thus, through Richards, Russell was kept completely informed of his target's activities. That included Preston's current full retirement and the buy-out and sell-off deals going on with his various holdings. His personal routine at Presthaven was covered in detail. Russell's interrogation never ceased.

Questions such as, "You're sure, no prostitutes?"

Richards' response is firm, "Absolutely not. If he was seeing any hookers on or off the estate, I'd know about it."

"So what the hell does he do with himself all day and night?"

Richards says, "He home tutors his grand daughter on the front porch week days from nine to four. I sometimes hear him telling her stories. The guy's had a fabulous life. But it looks like he's finally packed it in. At night he mostly just reads and drinks Scotch whisky neat in his study. Very sedentary. Rarely leaves the estate. When he does, I drive him."

Underwood questions further, "What about the daughter, Abigail?"

"Mostly stays close to home. She's seeing a shrink. Still broken up over her mother's murder and the loss of a husband years ago."

Russell muses, *Wonder what Dave would think if he knew I was the one who killed her mother? Maybe it worked out better that I didn't also do Abbey that night. This way she has more time to wallow in grief before I finally put her out of her misery.*

He asks, "And the kid?" Just to make sure all bases are covered.

Richards' answer reflects his fondness, "Little Miss Cassie Jean? She just had her eighth birthday party. Hardly ever leaves Presthaven. She's like Shirley Temple living on 'The Good Ship Lollypop'. Goes to school on the porch of a mansion. Plays croquet, takes tennis lessons. Swims, rides her pony. All right there on the estate. A black nanny named Gussie looks after her. If she goes out to another kid's party, I drive her and pick her up after. Doesn't act at all spoiled, though. She's a well mannered kid. Always says, "Thank you, 'Mr. Dave'.""

A psychopath's cynical thoughts: *What's with the '"Little miss Cassie Jean"? And she calls him "Mr. Dave"? How sweet. He should know how much I hate females, sweet or sour, any age. Precious little Cassie may have to seriously suffer, too.*

Attorney Underwood's careful accounting of Preston Dylan Jennings is over. He now turns to the matter of Savannah's appearance. He's gotten her a professional do-over. Skilled makeup artists have added more than a decade to her age. Shoulder length hair has been cut to the nape of her neck. Dyed to a softer color, touched-up with premature streaks of grey. His designers have fitted her with a fashionable, new, conservative but modestly sexy wardrobe. The beautiful ex-model can now pass for an extremely attractive forty-five year old woman.

Russell examines his associate's dramatically altered appearance and approves. Even as a girl, Savannah Lindstrom dreamed of being a seductive actress. She's now ready to visit the renowned Welshman himself. This will be the starring role of a lifetime.

CHAPTER 39

Mariposa lands on Cassie not at all like a delicate butterfly. A bee sting would be more like it.

It takes her only a minute to figure it out. *Manny and Gibby have steered you here to Tony!*

In fact, Manny had never lost touch with Tony the entire time he was away. He knew his old friend had returned from Italy last year. Tony was a money magnet over there, too. He'd renewed some old Mafia acquaintances in Palermo, Calabria and Sicily. In three years, he managed to accumulate a fortune in lire. That, combined with Manny's own club and cabaret resources, made them partners in the restaurant business. They opened DolceAmore six months ago to great success.

Manny then let his old friend, Detective Sergeant Mike Gibson in on a well-kept secret. The Vince Vega alias Tony Rosselli case was already closed as a suicide. Gibby, in Cassie's and PJ's best interests, let it stay that way. Then put together his modified witness protection plan.

Now, as Cassie continues to stare at a one word menu, PJ says, "Are you okay mom? You look like you put a finger in a light socket."

It was a shock alright. Before she can share the good news with PJ, the hostess reappears. "The owner would like very much to see you. Please follow me."

It's like that feeling she had when she got the million. Only better.

The hostess guides them to a back office. Tony is standing behind an antique Neapolitan desk. His arms are folded and there's a big, mustachioed grin on his face.

A surprised PJ blurts out, "Geez, is that you behind the 'stache, Tony?

Tony says, "Yep. Don't have anyplace else to be."

PJ laughs at that one. Then seizes the opportunity, "How 'bout we both be at Yankee Stadium?"

Tony's laughing now too, "Smart as ever, aren't you? You got it, pal. We'll sit right behind Don Mattingly at first base."

The man once known as Tony Roselli and Vince Vega is currently called Frank LaForge. He spots his St. Christopher medal on PJ's neck. It looks good on a newly reacquired son. That's the only time he has taken his eyes off Cassie. Surveying the latest dark-haired version of his wife, he gives her a wink, "Maybe we'll even bring your mom along." He says to her, "Do you like the name of the place?"

"DolceAmore? It's perfect. I love it."

"You better, I named it for you." His eyes hold hers, "Hello, Liz Harrison. A Cassie Jean by any other name would smell as sweet and look as beautiful."

Cassie returns his gaze, "I like your new looks, too."

It's true. It's been almost five years. At forty-three, he's older and more distinguished. Some men got even better looking with age. He was one of them. His curly hair is longer and greying at the temples. The mustache makes him look a lot like the actor Tom Selleck, whom she's been watching on her favorite TV show, "Magnum P. I.".

Tony opens his arms and she moves right in.

PJ crinkles his nose, *Yuk, here comes the lovey-dovey stuff. But geez, Tony's back! And finally, Yankee Stadium!*

CHAPTER 40

Back in Orlando, Lucas Wilson tries not to let the rhuematoid arthritis get the best of him as he lumbers towards all the noise at his front door. First, long rings, then loud, persistent banging. When Luke opens the door, he finds himself staring at two massive chests. Slowly lifting his head, he finds the faces of trouble.

A short guy, like him, steps out from behind two huge Mafia goons and shoves his way into the house. "We're lookin' for your former tenant. "By any chance, did she leave a forwarding address?"

Luke shakes his head and calmly answers, "No suh. Nevah did say."

Carmine Battaglia is an angry man. Payment on the Vince Vega invoice was long overdue.

He peels off two one hundred dollar bills and stuffs them in the waistline of of Luke's shorts, "It'd be very helpful if you could tell us where the girl went. Helpful to you, that is... it could help you not to get hurt. Do you get my drift?"

Lucas' pride outdoes his caution. He doesn't like bribes or threats. His eyes go to a place behind the corner cabinet. But the glance gives him away. Carmine points a chin towards where Lucas had taken his quick look. One of his men goes behind the cabinet and removes a 12 gauge waterfowl shotgun.

There is an expression of disappointment on Carmine's ruddy features. "That's not very hospitable. Or even wise, my black brother. Close quarters in here. You really wanna blow your place apart with a fuckin' shotgun?" His voice turns reasonable, "Look, all you hafta do is answer a simple question and we can still be friends."

Lucas is an uncomplicated man with no layers of deception. His thoughts are always close to the surface. With him, what you see is what you get. His answer is simple and direct, "Ah ain't yuh brotha and ah sho ain't yuh friend. Even if ah knowed where they was, ah still wouldn't tell y'all."

Carmine shakes his head, "That ain't nice, nigga." He looks at his men and says, "You try to be good to these people, but they got no respect for authority. We have to teach this arrogant spade a lesson. Show him how to be respectful." As their boss wanders through the little house looking for signs of a previous tenant, his men grab Lucas, rope him to a chair and take turns methodically slamming him with brass knuckles. He's beaten unconscious, then revived. His head is lifted and Carmine says, "Listen to me. All you gotta do is answer one easy question." His face is tight to Luke's, "Now, where the fuck is the broad?"

Luke's face is bloody from a broken nose and a mouth full of broken teeth. He manages to mumble through painfully swollen lips, "Maht as well kill me, muhfuckah. Ah ain't tellin' yuh nothin'."

His former tenants might as well be a daughter and grandson. He'd never betray them. Carmine, seething with frustration, reaches into Luke's waistline and removes the two bills. Then nods a go-ahead. Lucas is beaten again. Unmercifully. Until a proud, stubborn heart finally calls it quits. The fingers in his lap are folded in prayer.

Luke has given his life for Cassie and PJ. He died as he'd lived. Honorably.

CHAPTER 41

Savannah Lindstrom was a beautiful woman with an ugly secret.

Her expert makeover included horn-rimmed glasses over contact lenses that changed her eyes from green to hazel. A conservative suit with slacks hid curvy legs and the flats she wore reduced her height. Her naturally pale, nordic complexion was now two shades darker. Hair was shortened, dyed and restyled. All in all, it was an appearance befitting her role of a free-lance journalist seeking to write the biography of Preston Dylan Jennings.

She took the name Anna from the middle letters of her own Savannah, and adopted Alcott as a surname. Anna Alcott was on her ID. That's who she'd be from now on.

Her first and toughest test would be David Richards, Presthaven's Chief of Security. Avoiding recognition by Richards was crucial. He was a trained lawman. If anyone might see through her disguise, it would be him. And since he'd been hired, all phone calls and visits had to be made through him. There was no other way to get to Preston.

Even though Dave Richards was on Underwood's personal payroll, he could never be trusted to know their plan. Nor could he be expected to get involved with fraud, embezzlement and murder. Therefore, it was vital that he not recognize Anna Alcott or in any way connect her to Russell Underwood.

Russell kept daily track of Preston through his interrogations of Dave. One thing he didn't anticipate was the latter's resourcefulness in getting himself hired as Chief of Security at Presthaven. He couldn't deny it was a clever move that enabled Richards to be his eyes and ears on the inside. But it did create problems. Anna Alcott now had to get through him without being recognized. Beyond that, Richards was also on the Jennings payroll, creating a potential conflict of interest.

Thus, Russell had to develop a strategy to keep his inside man loyal while also explaining why he was hired to begin with. Richards was told Underwood had a business plan to buy some of Jennings' holdings, including Presthaven itself. The information he was gathering was essential to making the best possible deal. If the deal went through, there'd be an incentive for Dave. A bigger job and a big bonus.

Russell thinks, *That ought to keep him in my pocket. And from knowing the real reason he's working for me. Now it's a matter of Savannah getting past him to Preston.*

*   *   *

She has called ahead for an appointment. At the Presthaven gate house, Richards is now examining her credentials. *She's a journalist out of New York. Those horn rims make her look like a librarian. But a damned good looking one.* He has the vague notion of having met Ms. Alcott before, but can't quite place where or when.

He says, "Would you mind stepping out of the vehicle so I can search it, m'am?"

He sizes her up under that high collared blouse. *Nice boobs. No heels but still tall for a woman.* He lifts the rental Impala's trunk, finds it empty and goes through the rest of the interior. Checks her hand bag, finds only a small tape recorder and some note pads.

He smiles, "I never forget a face. Don't I know you from somewhere?"

Anna Alcott returns the smile, "I get that a lot. I'm one of those people who looks like other people. Mistaken for someone else all the time."

"Maybe I've seen your picture in the newspaper." Then jokes, "Or on a post office wall." He's reluctant to put to rest an inability to place her.

119

"You're a writer. Have I read anything you've written?"

"Probably not. I just do free lance stuff. I've written a novella but so far I'm an unpublished authoress." Her face is hopeful as she plays the sympathy card, "A biography of Preston Dylan Jennings is just what I need to establish my career as a serious writer."

Dave nods, finally picks up the intercom and says, "Miss Alcott is here to see you now, Sir."

Preston's voice crackles on the other end, "Send the lady in, Dave."

Presthaven's security chief and Russell's observer says, "Drive straight ahead, Miss Alcott. It's about a half mile to a circular driveway. You can't miss the mansion. Mr. Jennings will show you around. Very impressive place. Impressive man, too. You'll like him."

The big gates swing open. As she drives through, Savannah breathes a deep sigh of relief, *I'm sure he'll like me, too. Your bachelor days are numbered, Mr. Jennings.*

CHAPTER 42

Was she dreaming again? It was like those years of nights when she thought he was lost forever. He came to her then, too. But only in dreams.

Cassie now feels Tony standing over her in the darkness. He slips into bed, his hot body against hers, covering her mouth with his. Demanding, tongue-seeking kisses that immerse them in desire. Their hands move, finding each other's erogenous zones. His weight is on her, then hers on him. Her nipples hard enough to press into his cheeks and to welcome his lips. They roll over. He moves downward, kissing, tracing a path along her abdomen to her mons veneris. He spreads her thighs and flicks his tongue as she arches her pelvis. When they're both beyond ready, he slides onto her welcoming body, kisses her deeply and enters her.

Afterwards, they lay back on the bed in satiated silence. Both are thinking, *Even better than the last time on the honeymoon yacht.* That was over four years ago. Now they're together again and more determined than ever to stay that way.

Cassie looks around the lavish bedroom. Plush carpet. Pricey furniture. Floor to ceiling windows that overlook silver palms, a huge pool and a guest cabana. She still can't believe the home that Tony, now alias Frank LaForge, has been renting at a cost of $12,000 per month. The 5,000 square foot home has expansive views of Naples Bay and the Gulf of Mexico. It's situated on two acres of Gordon Drive in ritzy Port Royal.

But it was too much of a change from the modest Bonita Springs condo where PJ and she had been living. It's 1984 and now that they were together again, Cassie vowed to tone-down her husband's flamboyant life style. She wanted something less showy, with a lower profile. The Mafia, and God knows who else, would still be after them and the million.

It didn't take long for her cautious instincts to be confirmed with a phone call.

Tony is in the shower and can't answer. Cassie always had a sixth sense about bad news. She certainly had experienced enough of it in her life. She picks up the phone without speaking. The voice she hears is that of her friend and guardian, Detective Sergeant Michael Gibson.

He speaks carefully, "Is this Liz Harrison?"

"Yes, Gibby. It's me."

His tone is grave, "I hate to say it honey, but I've got some bad news for you. If you're standing, please sit down."

Bad news. Once again, her inner voice has proven correct. Granddaddy Preston always told her to trust the voice that speaks to her from inside. She says, "I'm sittin' Gibby. Talk to me."

Not knowing how to break the news easily, Mike Gibson simply says, "Luke died yesterday of a heart attack."

Cassie is stunned almost beyond words. She manages a weak, "Oh God, no."

Gibson reluctantly goes on, "Darlin', It wasn't just his heart that attacked him. He had a visit from the wiseguys who are still after your money." Then he adds, "They left a note for you."

CHAPTER 43

Cassie collects herself through the tears. She asks Gibby what the note said. He doesn't want to tell her. But she insists.

He replies, "Try not to worry too much about what it says. They don't know where or who you are anymore. You're safely undercover." Then he reluctantly reads, "This is what happens when you don't listen to reason. First Harry McIntyre. Then Lucas Wilson. Next, you, your kid and Vince unless you sign the money over."

By now, Tony is out of the shower and listening on an extension. He looks over at Cassie, who is sitting on the bed, trying to stay composed. He says to Gibby, "This is Frank LaForge. I thought you were retired, detective. How'd you find out about Lucas?"

Gibson answers, "I know who you are, Vega alias Roselli alias LaForge. The OPD Chief knew I was on your case. On Cassie's protection and PJ's recovery. I got a lotta history with you guys. So when Luke's body was found, I was informed." Gibby sighs, "It was Mafia alright. Three of them were seen by neighbors entering and leaving his house." He pauses, then says vehemently, "Wish I was still on the job to get those bastards. There was no better man than Luke."

Tony agrees, "Yeah, I know. He was the best. Maybe I'll kill the pricks myself."

Gibby cuts him short with sarcasm, "You've already committed suicide, dummy. Lets leave it at that. Best thing you can do is stay dead. And while you're deceased, remember to take care of your wife and son!"

Cassie jumps back into the conversation, "What about Luke's funeral?"

Gibson answers, " No funeral, hon. Just Potter's Field. A burial place for indigents and poor people with no family."

She counters, "That's not right. PJ and I are his family. He'll be buried decently in a real cemetery. And I'll be there for him. Count on it."

Both men quickly begin prevailing upon her. It would be foolish to arrange a burial, let alone be there when it happens. It's what they'll be looking for. She'd be playing right into Mafia hands. Wherever that cemetery was, whenever she'd be there, they'd be there, too.

But Cassie is adamant, "Luke is going into a decent cemetery and I'll be on hand to make sure he's properly prayed over. You guys think I don't know the Mafia will be there? So will the police. Disguised as cemetery employees, grave diggers, whatever."

Tony once called her a "delicate butterfly". But she was fast becoming an *iron* butterfly.

No, they won't talk her out of being the bait that catches Luke's killers. To Cassie, it's a matter of character. Her grandaddy once said, "Nobody can tell you who you are. That's something you must find out for yourself."

She's resolved to find out.

CHAPTER 44

Yes, Cassie Jean Dornwell has resolve. But so does Carmine Battaglia, Mafia Capo.

He didn't get to the top of the Casa Nostra in New Jersey for no good reason. But unlike his fictional counterpart, Tony Soprano, he had no soft spot. Even for his own family.

That was because he and wife Maria were childless when she died of cancer. At the time, he was distracted, got careless and let Vince Vega get away with mob money. Big bucks too. Vega not only got the million plus, but also took out two of his best men, including his primo hitter, Benjy "Big Hurt" Esposito.

Carmine was embarrassed. His highly regarded Capo reputation had been seriously undermined and was badly in need of restoration.

He was now hypothesizing. *The name won't be Vince Vega anymore. He already changed it once, to Tony Roselli. Whatever the name is now, he'd be back for that broad he married. She disappeared, but she's the key to Vince. And she won't ignore the burial of a landlord who'd die before he'd give her up. By killing him you now have the way to her.*

Battaglia, at age fifty, had a thirty-five year underworld education. He started as a numbers runner for Teamsters Local 560. He came to know Anthony, "Tony Pro" Provanzano, who later became a member of the Genovese crime family. Then, in 1975, Carmine became a minor Mafia legend by following the Teamster Union's boss Jimmy Hoffa to a restaurant in Bloomfield Township, Michigan. After that, Hoffa was never seen again. He worked his way up under Carlo Gambino, becoming

125

a made man as the result of whacking an enemy of "Bobby" Manna, head of the Hoboken crew. Manna and he later conspired to hit Capo di Tutti Capo (boss of bosses), John Gotti.

Gotti, who took over the Gambino Family and was known as the "Dapper Don" was resented by many in the Mafia. He was a preening showboat whose high profile antics in the '80s brought too much attention to his peers. Carmine was planning his own hit of Gotti, but that's when Vince Vega came into the picture to complicate his life.

Now Carmine's only obsession was finding Vega, his wife and the million. He was sure they'd gotten back together by now and were enjoying his money. The thought infuriated him. It was why he came from Jersey to Florida. He hated this place, especially now, in hot, humid August. But after his guys fumbled the ball, he had to come south himself. By now he'd already taken care of Harry McIntyre for crossing him and Lucas Wilson for refusing to answer a simple question.

He knew Cassie, her son and Lucas were a close-knit unit. They were together for over five years and Harry's reports said they were a solid family. That meant she'd be at the burial. And Vince would be there, too. No doubt Wilson's neighbors would also be there. But it didn't matter. In Vega and his wife, he had what he wanted.

Actually, he conjectured, *This is gonna be fun. Haven't been in the trenches for a long time. Really enjoyed being on the scene watching "Baby Face" Harry McIntyre go off the balcony and sending the old spade back to his slave ancestors.*

Murder without remorse was a fact of life for Carmine Battaglia. So was all the planning required to make sure that this time things were done right. He decided to take advantage of a semi-legitimate private sector acquisiton. It was a Paramus, New Jersey Waste Management and Recycling Company he'd bought four years ago. That connection would be used to execute the following plan:

Step One: He carefully reviewed obituaries in the Orlando Sentinel and other local newspapers. In doing so, he found the specifics of Lucas Wilson's burial. It is to take place next Tuesday. A graveside service will be held in the Chapel Hill Cemetery on Howell Road near Grove Street, where Lucas lived.

Step Two: Through his Jersey contacts, he leased a used Mack garbage collection and dump truck. It was a typically big, rear loader with a Cat 3000 engine and cart tippers. Then he had two magnetized signs fabricated. They would be applied to each side of the truck and would read: "D'Amato & Son Waste Disposal".

Step Three: He visited the director of Chapel Hill Cemetery. Made an offer of a month's free cleanup and removal that included the entire fifty acres of cemetery grounds. If their work was acceptable, D'Amato & Son will perform the same service for the next year at half the usual price. They'll be there to make the first cleanup and pickup on Tuesday.

It's an offer the Chapel Hill's director cannot refuse.

Step Four: He pulled his resources together. The massive twelve wheeler garbage truck will include weaponry and men as needed. Three of them will be in the empty dumpster and two will ride the rear bumpers. Carmine will be in the truck cab alongside the driver. Seven in all, armed and riding in a moving fortress.

He and his cleanup crew will arrive at 6 a.m., long before the 1 p.m. graveside ceremony. They'll work the grounds, find the grave site and be in the most advantageous position by the time the burial begins. In case there are cops, he has a backup plan. Most important, he and his soldiers will have the element of surprise in a virtual armored monster.

And there'll be no mistakes this time. He knows it's probably his last chance to redeem himself. When he gets his hands on Vega and the wife, he'll take back the mob's money along with his reputation. Once they sign over the million, he'll enjoy killing them.

CHAPTER 45

"A Man In Full" would have been the perfect title for the biography of Preston Dylan Jennings. Tom Wolfe took it for his novel thirty years later. But Savannah Lindstrom, alias Anna Alcott, hadn't thought of it when she was considering titles back in 1969.

It didn't matter, since the book she was writing was a sham anyway. Under the pretense of being a biographer, she'd wangled herself into Preston's confidence. A month of nights have been spent in his study interviewing him, taking notes, sharing his memories.

He teases her about doing a good job, "You'd better live up to that other Alcott... Louisa May."

She smiles at the reference. The name Alcott she'd adopted had once created quite a literary stir back in 1912 with the novel "Little Women".

She says, "That book was written two years after you came to America from South Wales. By then, you'd already made your first million."

"So you *have* been listening to me chattering away, after all." He smiles.

"Instead of "Little Women", she says, "Why don't we call this one 'Big Man'?"

He brushes off the heavy-handed flattery, "A better title would be 'Tired Old Man'."

She knows better. Not tired at all. On the contrary, still virile and wanting her. After nearly two months of a "professional" relationship, Anna Alcott's attire has gradually transformed from high bodices to lower necklines. From slacks to skirts that rise from mid-calf to the knee. Tied-back hair and horn-rimmed glasses are abandoned. The seduction is gradual and subtle. It's been seven years and counting since Preston has had a woman. And this particular woman is becoming more desirable with every passing evening. He wants to advance their relationship. But of course, she keeps him on the edge. There will be no sexual intimacy without a marriage commitment.

And finally, that's what she gets. Anna Alcott becomes Mrs. Preston Dylan Jennings twelve weeks after their first meeting. They are married in a simple ceremony on the Presthaven south lawn in the presence of Abigail and Cassie. Nanny Gussie and her husband Willie are witnesses.

On the other side of Florida, at the same moment the "I do's" are being exchanged, Russell Underwood is on the phone listening to Security Chief Dave Richards.

"Jennings is getting married as we speak. Damnedest thing, though. Sometimes the new wife looks like 'Marion the Librarian'. Other times, real sexy. Like an older sister of that model broad you got off for murder."

Underwood thinks, *He's getting too close. Now that the marriage mission has been accomplished, that erotic aura of hers has to be toned-down. Richards could start picking up the scent.*

CHAPTER 46

David Richards drove the Rolls Royce slowly so his passengers could comfortably enjoy Apopka's sights. Presthaven's Chief of Security and chauffeur was unaware of the irony.

Sitting in the back seat alongside the man he was hired to protect, was the biggest threat to that man's life.

Preston reached into the built-in bar of the customized Silver Cloud to serve his wife a drink. Anna Alcott Jennings sipped on a wine cooler as her husband pointed out the sights. There was the Gulf Oil facility he built in 1927. The town had literally risen up around it. As a result, Preston was considered by many to be Apopka's founding father.

They drove past Dream Lake, Old Dixie highway, restaurants and shopping malls. Nearly four decades of growth had turned a rural area into a suburban sprawl. But Preston and local community planners made sure the town's core retained an old Florida feel. There were still some narrow streets that were shaded by an arbor of Queen Palms. Compared to nearby Orlando in the sixties, Apopka was an anachronism. To Savannah however, small town charm had little appeal. She much preferred modern Miami, a city that was second only to Las Vegas for its tacky, glitzy come-on.

Even better, was the cosmopolitan ambience of New York City. She daydreamed of shopping at Saks and Tiffany when the money was hers.

Their marriage was now six months old and she thought things were going well. But the union was standing on the shaky foundation of a twelve week courtship and hairline cracks were beginning to show. For one thing, since his new wife came to live in Presthaven, there was a cordial but lacking in warmth relationship with daughter Abigail and granddaughter Cassie. He supposed he'd have to give her time, but hoped there would be more family intimacy by now. For another thing, she seems to have lost her enthusiasm for biography writing.

And then there was the strangely forceful sex. Passionate yes, but not at all the truer, gentler love making he had with Betsy. Savannah, even under her assumed identity, was still an impatient, demanding lover. During sex, there'd be no slow, romantic moonlight sonatas. She preferred intense, exotic music. The driving chords of Ravel's "Bolero" were more suited to the heavier rhythm of her body atop his. She always assumed the superior position, pounding him with a fury that would have exhausted a younger man.

Preston tried to make a joke out of it, "Slow down Annie; enjoy the ride. Hell, I'm almost eighty. What are you trying to do, give an old man a heart attack?"

CHAPTER 47

Another few months went by. Preston had come to realize there was an apt description for sex with his new wife: "dispassionate passion".

During the extreme intimacy of sex, he never felt more distanced from her. And with each passing week, her beautiful face would gradually become that of a stranger.

When he was alone, he'd gaze at another familiar countenance on the desk of his study. It was the last picture taken of Betsy at age sixty. Her face, framed by silver hair, was smiling at the lens of his camera. His first wife was not as conventionally beautiful as Anna Alcott Jennings, but somehow far lovelier.

Preston once told Cassie, "Sometimes, life can be hell on the way to heaven." She would soon find that out. But for now, Preston was on that journey himself. He'd foolishly committed to a woman without really knowing her. What's more, over the past few months he was losing his usual zest and physicality. Increasing headaches and lethargy had entered his life. He imagined it was just because he was getting old.

But there was a better reason. Savannah had given up on killing him with coitus. Besides, sex was becoming more and more infrequent. But healthy body cells were being compromised. The steady, untraceable dosages of arsenic, as dictated by Russell Underwood, were slowly taking effect.

*   *   *

On a September Tuesday in 1984, retired Detective Sergeant Michael

Gibson is kissing his wife Adrienne goodbye. He's about to leave Orlando for St. Petersburg. Adrienne gives her husband an exasperated shake of the head, "When are you going to quit the job for real?"

Gibson holds her in has arms and says, "This is it, I promise. But I gave Cassie my word I'd be there for her. She's gonna need all the help she can get today."

"I know you think of her as family, but you do have one of your own. A wife, daughters, grandchildren. You have an obligation to us, too. Stay alive, dammit."

His loving wife of forty years knows too well of her husband's sense of duty and honor. She loves him for it, but hoped that after a year of retirement, he could get the job out of his system. She has strong misgivings this time. But there's no arguing with him when he's made up his stubborn Irish mind.

She kisses him goodbye while she locks the clasp of a St. Christopher medal around his neck, "Keep it there. I have a feeling you're going to need it."

Meanwhile, Cassie Jean Dornwell, alias Elizabeth Harrison is preparing for the cemetery burial of her good friend, Lucas Wilson. Husband Tony Roselli, alias Frank LaForge, is dressing beside her. They are obviously concerned with what lies ahead. Twelve year-old PJ will be left behind with a trusted friend. There is eminent danger in their visit to Chapel Hill Cemetery in Orlando. By her own choice, Cassie will be the bait police use to capture Luke's killers.

They leave Naples at 8 a.m. for a burial to take place at one o'clock. Gibby, who wouldn't miss this showdown for the world, will meet them in St. Petersburg, halfway there. They'll park their car, get into his and use the driving time to review the cemetery scenario. He's ready for action, packing his .38. Tony has his Glock. As long as PJ is safe at home, Cassie is confident. Her own weapon is her resolve.

As they drive northeast on Route 4, Carmine Battaglia and his lethal crew are already at work cleaning up Chapel Hill's fifty acres. Two hours later, at 10 a.m., four unmarked police cars, each with a two man team, are positioned at various points on the cemetery grounds. They ignore the working garbage truck and watch the front gates for suspicious visitors. In turn, they are observed by the Mafia as a police stakeout.

At 11 a.m., Carmine dispatches a stealth sniper on foot to render the inhabitants of each parked, unmarked police car ineffective. The trained, ex-GI marksman will achieve his objective by firing an AK-47 rifle equipped with a silencer and non-lethal bullets. These heavily rubberized projectiles deliver victims only into unconsciousness. The Mafia doesn't mind eliminating an occasional ordinary citizen, but retribution for police killings is to be avoided.

The sniper fires from strategically hidden positions eight times with unerring accuracy. All policemen in all four vehicles have been rendered unconscious. Two mafia men then change places with the occupants of one of the cars, donning their uniforms.

Carmine warns his men that his quarry must be taken alive. Ever since bank insider Harry McIntyre went off that balcony, the Mafia boss had no way of knowing where the money was secretly transferred.

If all goes well, firepower from the garbage truck will only be needed as a threat. Cassie and Tony will be "rescued" by the Mafia-occupied police vehicle when they are threatened by men in the truck with guns.

At half past noon, Gibby, Cassie and Tony move through the gates of Chapel Hill Cemetery. Several of Luke's friends and neighbors are arriving as well. Carmine watches everyone through binoculars from his command post in the truck cab. As they leave their car and walk to the grave site, he spots his targets with no difficulty.

A rush of thoughts, *They're here! Both of them. Still got the old instincts. Cops set a trap, like you figured. But now they're sleeping on the job. This is your last, best chance.*

He loves the adrenalin rush, "Okay boys, let's go get 'em."

At 1p.m., the worshippers gather around a priest who stands alongside

Luke's coffin at graveside. The priest consecrates the grave and intones the antiphon. As the coffin is lowered, the rumble of a Mack collection and dump truck is heard approaching. Gibby looks up and sees several men standing astride the huge vehicle.

Their automatic weapons are pointed towards all who are solemnly gathered at graveside.

CHAPTER 48

It's now only minutes before the graveside ceremony is to take place. Cassie, a film buff, thought how such sad scenes were depicted in movies. It was always raining.

It wasn't raining, but it wasn't a typically bright Florida day, either. Bad weather is definitely on its way. At 1 p.m., the sky is getting darker, to fit her mood. Cassie stands beside Tony reflecting on Lucas and what a good, kind man he was. Never asked for rent money when she was late with it. Never accepted payment for sitting PJ. There would be no Potters Field for Luke. She is determined to avenge his death right here, where the police can capture his killers.

When Cassie first hears the rumblings of the garbage truck that barrels towards them, she thinks it's distant thunder. A prelude to the wind and rain that was surely coming. After all, it's September, hurricane season. But the only storm about to hit graveside was man-made. Tony grabs her protectively as he sees the gunman on the big truck and hears a familiar voice booming out. Carmine Battaglia is standing on the front cab running board and shouting, "Nobody move."

Retired Detective Michael Gibsons' first reaction is to draw his sidearm, but quickly reconsiders. He hopes Tony will use the same caution. *A lot of innocent people can get hurt if these Mafia guys see the flash of a gun. There's a shit load of firepower on that truck.*

Carmine points at Cassie and Tony, "You two. Walk towards me with your hands up over your head."

As they step forward, Tony is thinking, *Where the fuck are all the*

136

cops? Be ready to hit the dirt with Cassie if and when they show up. Meanwhile, Gibby muses, *A garbage truck. Smart. Probably here before the stakeout and got overlooked. But where the hell are the good guys now? There were supposed to be at least four cars and eight cops.*

Just then, as Cassie and Tony stand in the road with their arms raised, one of the unmarked police cars, with a hand-placed magnetized roof light flashing, comes screeching from out of nowhere. It pulls up between them and the truck. A rear door is thrown open as a uniformed "cop" jumps out. He pushes them into the vehicle and fires his .38 special over the truck. He then jumps back in the car as it speeds off. Automatic weapons fired from the truck whiz harmlessly above the police vehicle.

The crowd reacts to a daring rescue by the cops. But Gibby knows better. He immediately makes it for an elaborate ruse and dashes for his car. Carmine's men see him, but figure it's just someone running away in panic. Now that they've achieved their objective, they don't pay much attention as he jumps into his car and races out of the cemetery.

Gibby drives to catch up with the standard police issue Chevrolet, but can't get too close. He needs to follow without detection. They'll be taking Cassie and Tony to a place where they will meet up with Battaglia.

He follows the Chevy traveling south on Route 27, keeping it in sight at a respectful distance through a scrim of showers. He reaches for his cell phone wishing he was in his old squad car equipped with a police radio. When he dials OPD to advise them of his pursuit, the only response he gets is static. Meanwhile, the sound of thunder and flashes of lightning accompany a sudden gust of wind and heavy rain. It's a typical September squall that makes it difficult to drive, let alone follow another vehicle at eighty miles an hour.

Hunched over the wheel, eyes straining through hammering rain and dancing windshield wipers, Gibby is having an animated conversation with himself.

Another fine mess you got yourself in, Ollie. Adrienne's right. You can take the cop off the job but you can't take the job off the cop.

CHAPTER 49

It's a hellish storm. Pouring rain that seems to accelerate by the second. Explosive flashes of lightening. Bursts of wind. As he cuts through it, Gibson's Taurus keeps swaying sideways. Visibility is practically zero as he thinks, *Thank God they never took their roof flasher off*. He follows the red flasher and spots a green and white highway sign that blurs by. He can barely read it: Lake Ockeechobee 120 miles.

In the police vehicle ahead, Tony is holding Cassie's hand and asking, "Where are we going to meet Carmine?" They've known for over an hour that they're not in the protection of police. Soon after leaving the cemetery, Tony was relieved of his Glock at gunpoint.

The "cop" driver answers Tony's question with amused sarcasm, "We're goin' to a nice little vacation spot in the Everglades. Lots of amenities for ya... mosquitos, swamps, quicksand. To say nothin' of the snakes and crocs."

                    *   *   *

Carmine Battaglia has decided to stay in Orlando and sit out the storm. At least they're not forecasting a hurricane. His men will drive him down to the Everglades early tomorrow morning when the weather clears. His Florida connections had put him in touch with some "local talent" down there. Good ol' cracker boys who will assist with guarding, then torturing his captives. After the money is signed over, they die. The Everglades is a great place to get lost forever.

Gibby checks his watch. It's been almost five hours of driving through the storm when he finally leaves the highway and follows the unmarked police car onto a remote dirt road. They are now on the southern edge of Lake Ockeechobee. He pulls off to the side about thirty yards away and watches through the driving rain as they are met by a dark-skinned, muscled guy in a soaked shirt and a red bandana. There are also two other spooky-looking dudes.

The one in the bandana is a third generation half-breed Seminole named "Indian Joe". He heads up the welcoming committee for Carmine's visitors. The others are twin brother albinos known by locals as "Gator" and "Frog". Due to their congenital condition, they are lifetime inhabitants of the Everglades. The absence of skin pigmentation encourages them to avoid sun from the outside world.

Leaving the Chevy where it's parked, the fake cops hustle Cassie and Tony out and push them along, following Indian Joe into the mangroves. Gibby watches from his Taurus and ponders the next move.

Daylight is starting to abandon them as they make their way through the mosquito and snake infested Everglades. Indian Joe leads the way and the albino brothers bring up the rear. Cassie glances back at them and shivers. With that ghostly white skin and those blazing pink eyes, they are straight out of a monster movie. As she struggles through swamp cabbage and saw grass to keep up with the others, she feels like she's living in a slow-motion nightmare.

Two miles from where they started, the travelers arrive muddy, bleeding from saw grass cuts and exhausted. Their destination is a decaying "stilt house". Four corner stilts are required to both support and raise the structure above its swampy foundation. To gain entry, Indian Joe motions his four visitors across planks and up a flight of rotting steps.

He pulls Cassie aside to wait for the others to enter first. When it's her turn to climb, he gets behind her, reaches up with both hands and roughly squeezes her buttocks. She turns to take a swipe at him. He laughingly avoids it and says, "Calm yerself sweetie. And get used to it! Dat purty ass a yers belongs to me an mah boys now."

Cassie thinks, *The real nightmare now begins.*

CHAPTER 50

Retired Detective Sergeant Michael Gibson has a difficult choice.

Should he break into the parked squad car and use the police radio? Or follow Cassie, Tony and their captors into the Everglades?

He opts for the latter and sets out after them, thinking, *If you don't tail them through this godforsaken wilderness, you might never see them again*. He moves slowly and keeps his distance, following the noise as they plow their way through muddy marshes and belligerent, jungle-like growth. He swears silently, *Now you know why they call it "sawgrass". Fuckin' stuff cuts like a serrated blade*.

It seems to take forever before the sounds ahead come to a stop. Moving stealthily forward, he crouches behind a big palmetto bush and watches them ascend into a rickety old place sitting on stilts at the edge of the mangrove. The albinos, who wait in guard with shotguns outside, are discussing what Indian Joe said to Cassie.

Gibby got there just in time to hear it...

"Dat purty ass a yurs belongs to me and mah boys now."

He's hidden himself at a distance but within earshot, listening in on the albino brother's conversation.

Gator gloats, "Y'hear that Frog? We gonna get some a that action, too. Sloppy seconds afta Joe gits through wit' her."

Gibby shudders as Frog answers, "Yeah bro, why don't we double up on the bitch? Let's flip a coin. Heads yuh got the front, tails the back."

Rain is finally letting up, but night is falling fast. Gibson knows if he tries to make it to the car radio for help, and then back, he risks getting lost in a jungle labyrinth. Then what happens if Indian Joe and monster men get at Cassie? No choice but to stay here. He can't expect help from Tony, either. They're sure to have him tied up good.

So, he thinks, *You're on your own, just like you were when you got PJ back. But that was a walk in the park compared to this.*

Lights are now on in the shack. There's no glass in the windows, just screening against bugs and mosquitos. Gibby can hear as well as see some of what's going on inside. He listens to the voices of Indian Joe and the two wiseguys. Nothing from Tony or Cassie. They're probably gagged.

But he learns a lot from the others. They have talked to Carmine from the car. He'll be here in the morning. He won't want to stay long. He insists on directing the torture. After he gets what he wants, the albino brothers can dump their bodies somewhere in the swamp. Meantime, in his own words, "Have fun."

The mob guys and Indian Joe are now arguing.

The half Seminole grins, "Rape is havin' fun. I say we do her tonight."

The first mafiaso counters, "That tied-up burlap bag full of rattle snakes you put in her room is fun enough." He says, "Fun don't have to include rape. I ain't sure the boss would go for it."

His counterpart objects, "What's more fun than rape? There ain't nothin' else to do waitin' in this fuckin' shit hole. It's you against the Injun and me, right, chief?"

Indian Joe nods, "Majority rules. We draw straws for who goes first."

Cassie and Tony are tied up, blindfolded and gagged in two separate rooms, but there's nothing covering their ears. Gibby is listening too.

And sharing the trepidation. The sixty-one year old retired cop is now full of self-doubt. *With these freaks guarding the place and three more up there inside, there's no way. But it's Cassie, for Christ's sake. At least you gotta try.*

Squatting behind the Palmetto with his feet sinking ankle-deep in the bog, he drops to his knees and looks heavenward, *While you're down here, you might as well pray for a miracle.*

CHAPTER 51

There could be no more disparity of environs in the entire State of Florida than the Everglades and Presthaven.

But paradise that it is, Presthaven has become a bore to Savannah Lindstrom. During the year she's lived as Anna Alcott Jennings, ennui has set in. Besides the apathy, she's grown impatient waiting for her husband to die.

She hasn't been able to stop his heart with the forceful sex that has finally ended. And the arsenic doled out in such small doses by Russell's edict, is taking forever to accomplish her objective. She does notice some increased lethargy. But the old man still spends six hours every weekday, tutoring his grand daughter. He continues to slow-ride his horse on Presthaven's back acres. And still sits in his study until early morning, taking his Cutty Sark, neat.

Toughness got Preston through a most eventful and productive life and he will not go easily into the hereafter.

Frustration crosses Savannah's perfect features as she asks herself, *How much waiting can you do? How much swimming, sitting by the pool and being bored to death?*

The lawn games, tennis and horseback riding offered at Presthaven have never been her thing. But shopping during the day, big city lights at night, cafe cruising, dancing and drinking definitely are. She's always thrived on action and sex. Which is why she had once lived in Miami. That was where she met, married and murdered her husband, Ben Murcer.

She was now returning there with regularity. Her long, exciting weekends are a welcome change from the mundane Presthaven.

Meanwhile, during her weekend excursions, Preston has taken to some intellectual pursuits beyond home-schooling Cassie. Dissatisfaction had generated suspicion. He's been gathering his attorneys for a look into his wife's past. It's time to re-examine his situation and re-structure his last will and testament.

Preston's lawyers were unable to find birth records. Or for that matter, any solid background material at all on the previous life of Anna Alcott. The ID she carries is forged and she appears to be nothing she purports to be. When they inform him of the apparent scam, the venerable tycoon takes it as a bitter lesson learned.

He smiles ruefully and immediately accepts the blame, *You let your emotions trump your good sense. Should have had her investigated right up front. You were just a lonely old fool who confused flattery and sex with love and marriage.*

He decides to say nothing to Anna until he's remade his will and divested himself of the vast majority of his wealth. Only Abigail, Cassie and her nanny Gussie, will be major inheritors. The remainder of his money is to be distributed to charities all over Florida. He'll return the lion's share of his fortune to where it was made. And his revamped philanthropy will soon rival that of the Vanderbilts, Mellons and Carnegies.

Upon his demise, even the property that comprises Presthaven itself, will be gifted. He's selected a most worthy beneficiary. An entrepreneurial Welshman named Malcolm Crothers, who reminds him of his younger self. The fellow runs a worthy business, building convalescent facilities. The gift will be pending the approval of daughter Abbey, whenever she and Cassie are ready to move into a smaller, more manageable residence.

Preston has one more task for his attorneys... they are to draw up divorce papers.

When he's ready to confront his wife, she'll learn the consequences of her deception. With a smile of satisfaction, he contemplates, *Anna Alcott, or whoever the hell you are, you're an arrogant, greedy woman who married only for money. And soon you'll have your just reward. Not a dime from me. But incarceration for you.*

Preston made an error in judgement thirty-five years ago when he didn't have another family member, a son-in-law, thrown into jail. He won't make the same mistake twice.

There is, of course, an irony involved. The people who have taken part in both instances, are partners in crime. And are determined to take his life along with his money.

CHAPTER 52

There are 4,000 square miles of Florida Everglades containing several ecosystems. And millions of birds, from Barred Owls to Bald Eagles. Thousands of mammals, from Black Bears to Panthers. There are reptiles unchanged in appearance for 250 million years. It's the only spot on Planet Earth where Crocodiles and Alligators coexist in the same habitat.

A truly unique part of the world. But the last place Mike Gibson wants to be tonight.

It's still raining and the moon is hidden behind storm clouds in this isolated area of jungle-like marshland. Therefore, the only light source comes from the dilapidated shack that sits on stilts at the edge of a mangrove.

It is guarded by the albino twins, Gator and Frog. They have pump-action shotguns at their sides. The lack of moonlight perfectly suits their aversion to anything bright. From Gibby's sightline, kneeling in the darkness, the ambient light from the shack above casts an eerie glow. It transforms them into milky apparitions with unnaturally glowing eyes.

As such, they are a truly frightening sight. But fortunately, since he's out of the lit perimeter, they can't see him. Darkness is his only friend out here. It's all he has to execute his strategy. That is, if you can call hoping, praying and waiting, a strategy.

*　　　　*　　　　*

Meanwhile, within the stilt house, Tony is struggling with his bonds. He's locked in a toilet and tied to the commode plumbing. What the degenerate bastards are planning for Cassie enrages him. He's always had a short fuse, but this anger is beyond anything he's ever known. It's producing adrenaline-induced strength. If his arms and legs were bound with ordinary rope he might have broken free by now. But he's tied expertly by Indian Joe with incredibly strong mangrove vines.

In the adjoining bedroom, a terrified Cassie is praying to the patron saint of travelers, *Please, St. Chris, bring Tony and me back home safely to PJ.* She sits in bed, arms over her head, elbows up, hands tied to a headboard rail. *One rape in a lifetime is enough, thank you. If ganddaddy were here he'd say don't panic, use your head.*

He once told her, "The way you use whatever you have, no matter how little, determines your character and your success." Of course he meant it as a life lesson. But she realizes that right now she does have something that may be of use. It's flimsy and small and has never been thought of as a weapon. But it's all she has. If she keeps her head and promises not to resist, they might untie her hands so she can get at it.

She can now hear a racket being made by the winner of the "straw vote". Indian Joe is just outside the bedroom laughing, "Sorry guys, but after ah's done with her, she'll be unfit fer the rest a yuh."

When the bedroom door opens, she tries her best to hide her revulsion. He fills the doorway, stark naked except for his red bandana. Cassie forces a seductive smile, stares at his phallus and says, "My, how big. Can I touch it?"

The Seminole devours the flattery. He was planning on simply brutalizing her. But now he wouldn't mind some cooperative foreplay at all. He says, "If ah let yuh touch, will yuh know what to do wid it?"

She half whispers, "Why don't you close the door and give us some privacy. Then come over here and find out for yourself."

Joe shuts the bedroom door and approaches, grinning and proud of his flagrant manhood. He leans over the bed, tears her blouse open and rips off her bra. She shivers but masks her fright as sexual excitement.

Fondling her bare breasts, he says, "Nice. Jus' the way ah like 'em. Firm and not too big."

Knowing the only way this will work is to fall quickly into role play, she groans softly. "Your hands feel good, Joe. I'm sure my nipples have told you that already. But now I want to return the favor. Let me hold onto that big boy you got down there."

He can hardly contain himself as he releases her hands from the headboard rail.

But not without a warning, "Be nice and don't try nothin' stupid, bitch. Rememba, ahm a crazy half-breed that's very good wid a knife. Yuh wouldn't want me to cut up that purty face a yurs."

Cassie responds, "No worries hon. Let's get it on."

She reaches down for him with her left hand and finds the metal clip in her hair with the right. While holding his erection in one hand, she grasps the pried-open hair clip in the other. Then, with all the strength she has left, simultaneously stabs and twists it deeply into his left eye socket.

Fatal trauma to the eye results. Sclera attaching extrinsic muscles that move the eyeball are ripped apart. As vessels burst, blood and vitreous humor jelly gush forth. With his sight orb hanging out of its socket via only a few strands of cilia, Indian Joe lets out a primal, high-pitched scream.

CHAPTER 53

The ungodly scream is the diversion Gibby's been waiting for. His only strategy was to rush the albinos the minute they were distracted.

He now has the advantage of surprise, coming at them out of darkness. He fires his .38 as he runs forward. His first shot goes wide but the second hits Frog in the chest and drops him, mortally wounded. Gator gets off reflexively fast return fire that explodes into a cypress over his attacker's head. Before he has a chance to pump the rifle for another shot, Gibby spins him sideways with a bullet to the shoulder. Then another in the head.

Meanwhile, all hell is breaking loose in the shack. The two wiseguys hear the gunfire outside and scramble for their weapons. At the same time, Cassie comes running out of the bedroom as Indian Joe, still screaming, weaves after her. The nude Seminole, his face now a mask of blood that matches his bandana, goes immediately to where his twenty inch Condor Machete rests by the front door. Half blind, but totally maniacal, he advances on Cassie with his deadly weapon.

He gets a warning from one of the mob guys, "Stop right there, you naked, dick-swingin' half-breed. Carmine wants her alive."

But his caveat is ignored as Joe shoves past him and heads for Cassie on the other side of the room. She's run out of space and is cowering in the corner, trying to hold her torn blouse together.

The enraged half-breed doesn't hesitate, "I don't give a fuck what you wops want. What I want is to kill the bitch. She took out my eye!"

He reaches Cassie, who is now curled in a fetal position on the floor. Standing over her, Indian Joe raises the machete above his head. Just as the big blade is about to flash down, he screams yet again as he takes a bullet in the back.

The second Mafioso looks at his partner and shrugs, "It ain't as though you didn't warn the crazy, one-eyed sonofabitch. That's one Injun that got too far off the fuckin' reservation."

*   *   *

Gibson is now crouched on a wobbly step outside and just under the front door of the shack. He's lucked out so far, but that was on the ground below, under cover of darkness. Up here, he figures his chances of getting inside alive are somewhere between slim and none.

He then hears the shot fired at Indian Joe and the mobster's subsequent comments. He takes assessment, *Okay, one down. Two to go. The odds are getting better.*

He waits patiently, listening for further conversation and another opportunity. More voices now, and a turn of the door knob. The Mafia men are wondering about the shots fired outside.

One of them says, "Lemme find out." He opens the door and shouts into the darkness below, "Hey Gator, Frog. What the fuck were you guys shootin' down there? Target practice... or Panthers?

He gets no answer but does get a hand around his ankle. Gibby yanks hard, sending him out the door and richocheting off the steps into the swamp below. He lands hard and starts sinking into muck. Gibson cranes his neck, searching in semi-darkness. He can barely make out the mobster's body as it slowly disappears into a morass of black quicksand.

The retired detective breaths a heavy sigh of relief. Only one bad guy left. He knows how incredibly fortunate he is to have gotten this far. And from what he can surmise, Cassie is still alive, if not exactly well.

Thank the Lord, he thinks, kissing the medal around his neck. But he wonders how long this kind of luck can last.

Within the next few seconds, he'll find out.

As he shifts his head from the disappearing act below to the doorway above, the retired cop finds himself looking directly into the muzzle of a Smith & Wesson 500 magnum revolver.

The one mobster left is standing not six feet away, on the open threshold. He's aiming the business end of his weapon right between Gibby's eyes. The second the Mafioso pulls the trigger, Gibby knows his life is over.

CHAPTER 54

But instead of where it's aimed, the bullet catches his left ear, tearing it away. The explosion from such close range is deafening and he will never hear out of that ear again. But it's not the kill shot intended. Even in shock, Gibby wonders why he's not dead.

It's because Cassie, just recovered from her own near demise, has scrambled off the floor and rushed across the room from behind the gunman. Her outstretched arms push him forward, changing the direction of his shot and sending him hurtling down over Gibson's head. He lands face first with a loud thud and gets quickly sucked under, joining his partner in hell.

The beleaguered young mom then helps haul her wounded friend up from the steps and into the shack. She immediately finds a disinfectant. There are several "good-ol'-boy" bottles of Jack Daniels laying around. She grabs one and pours alcohol over Gibby's open wound, disinfecting it while causing a loud yelp. She then rips her torn blouse into strips and wraps them around his head, creating a tight compress.

He hurts like hell and his head is reverberating as he catches the grisly sight of Indian Joe's face with its missing orb. *So that's what caused the blood-curdling scream.* Gibby's ear is gone but his cop's sense of black humor is still intact, "I'm glad you kept an eye out for me, hon."

Cassie, shuddering, just wants to forget the horror.

Then it dawns on her she's now immodestly topless. Gibby notices, too. He gallantly removes his own shirt and hands it to her. Even with his head booming, he gives her a weak smile and a wink, "It's not that I don't appreciate the view. Believe me, you wouldn't get the shirt off my back if you didn't save my life."

Cassie returns a smile of appreciation to the man she has come to regard as a foster father. Meanwhile, Tony is still stuck in the toilet, bound to the commode and shouting like a wild man, "What the fuck is going on out there? It sounded like World War Three. But am I right? Are you two somehow okay and those bastards gone?"

Now that the horror show is over, Cassie can finally exhale. "You heard right, honey. Gibby and I are still here and the bad guys are dead and gone. Everythin' is under control. But I must say, you do spend a lot of time in the bathroom."

They are still laughing as she cuts him loose with the late Indian Joe's machete. The latter is then unceremoniously thrown out the door by Tony to join his companions in the mucky graveyard below.

Now they have a long night ahead to give thanks for a miraculous survival and to make plans for still another deadly encounter. They should get Gibby to a hospital, but haven't a chance of navigating these dense mangroves without a guide. There's no choice but to await until morning for Carmine and his deadly friends.

CHAPTER 55

David Richards, Presthaven's Chief of Security is on the phone with his boss. "Lots of lawyers in and out of here for the last three weeks."

Russell Underwood listens carefully and says, "Check the gate house log. Is it the same legal firm every time?"

"Yep, Carter, Togias and Hill. They're only logged in Fridays, Saturdays and Sundays. Weird, lawyers working on weekends, huh? But that's the way Preston Dylan Jennings wants it. And he's got the moola to get what he wants."

Gears are turning, "Tell me about Mrs. Jennings. What's she doing while they're with her husband?"

Richard's says, "She's not here. Spends long weekends in mostly Miami, sometimes Palm Beach. Leaves early Friday, gets back on Monday"

Underwood thinks, *When we talk on the phone she never mentions these excursions of hers. Only says Preston's not dying fast enough and she's getting bored. She's obviously been going out on spending sprees and more... the night action she's always craved. Reverting to old habits. And Jennings pays the bills. By not staying put, the bitch has jeopardized everything.*

He says, "Does she tell you where she goes?"

"Naw, just takes off in that yellow Corvette convertible of hers. Living the good life of a rich wife. But I do know where she goes. When she gets back I see valet parking stickers from the Boca Raton Resort Club and shopping bags from Saks Fifth Avenue. She stays at Fisher Island or the Fontainbleau. Shops in Coconut Grove. Nothin' but the best."

Russell can easily imagine it. *She's back to her old ways. Day-long shopping sprees. Cocktail hours and four-star restaurants. Midnight cruises on the Intercoastal. No doubt fucking her escorts bow-legged.*

The brilliant Underwood mind is now racing at warp speed, *Preston senses he doesn't have long to live and is adjusting his will. He only meets with his lawyers when his wife is away. The man's no fool. He's obviously unhappy with the deceitful bitch.*

Then another, more alarming thought occurs, *The lawyers may be drawing up divorce papers already!*

He says to Richards, "Give me the names of the attorneys from Carter, Togias and Hill."

His informant checks the gate house log book. "Let's see, looks like it's always the same three... Jason Carter, Senior Partner. Marjorie Verty, Associate. Ralph Gorda, Paralegal.

Russell immediately targets the latter, basically an intern. Ralph Gorda will help him identify one of Preston's philanthropic recipients. He needs a name. And he needs it fast.

CHAPTER 56

Ralph Gorda didn't see any real harm in it. The guy simply wanted to know who might some day be the beneficiary of Presthaven. And he paid the handsome sum of five thousand dollars to find out.

That's a lot of dough to a low-salaried intern at Carter, Togias and Hill. Especially for a name that would never matter. After all, the will said Preston Dylan Jennings' daughter Abigail would have to approve such a gift. There was no way a still relatively young woman would agree to give away such a beautiful, valuable home.

Five thou was too much to pay for virtually worthless information. But the guy could obviously afford it. Said he knew Jennings from way back and was just curious as hell about who outside the family might get the place. Even if it was twenty years from now.

Gorda met with Russell in Lake Buena Vista for the exchange. He traded what he assumed was useless information for a manilla envelope containing ten $500 Federal Reserve Notes.

*   *   *

Russell Underwood had traveled from Tallahassee to Orlando the day after he spoke on the phone with Dave Richards. The name he bought from Ralph Gorda was worth millions beyond the five thousand he'd paid for it. That name was The Crothers Group, Inc., an LLC not yet listed on the New York Stock Exchange.

Russell researched The Crothers Group and found a small, struggling company barely able to meet its payroll. They are developers in the ALF

(Assistant Living Facility) business. Their CEO's name is Malcolm Crothers, a young Welshman who founded the company only two years ago, when he became a U.S. citizen and resident of Florida. It was easy to see why Preston would select such a sympathetic beneficiary.

Crothers not only had the same birthplace but also the entrepreneurial bent that drove Preston fifty years earlier. He had high hopes of achieving success in the field of health and rehabilitation. The Florida population was skewed to advanced age and was a good market for nursing homes. But the costs of a start-up company were proving to be a difficult challenge. At this point in time, Malcolm Crothers was badly in need of financing.

That's what he got from Russell Underwood, who purchased controlling interest in his firm for 1.2 million dollars with another half million to Malcolm Crothers himself. A condition of the deal was that the stock purchase be kept quiet. Crothers would remain CEO of the company that Underwood would now own. All in all, the young Welshman felt lucky to net an amount in excess of what he felt was his firm's current value.

But Russell knew better. In less than a year, The Crothers Group would be worth ten times what he paid for it. Of course, he wasn't interested in the company itself, only Presthaven. As soon as he held title to the land, he'd sell off Crothers Group and keep Presthaven for himself.

*   *   *

Having completed a transaction of such vital importance, Russell's thoughts turned to Savannah, *That greedy, self-indulgent bitch ruined the plan. Jennings will now doubtless change his will. The money he's alloted for family will no longer include a wife. He might even have her locked up for fraud and attempted embezzlement.*

Now the Underwood master plan must be seriously altered. The first move was the immediate acquisition of The Crothers Group. Mission accomplished. Next, he must use Savannah to assist him in an entirely new scenario regarding Preston.

He calls on her cell, "I'm coming to visit you tomorrow in Presthaven."

She responds, "Have you gone mad? You can't be seen here, it would ruin everything!"

"You may have already accomplished that. I've come to the conclusion that your husband is on the verge of divorcing you."

Russell hears the sharp intake of Savannah's breath. Recovering, she says, "I don't believe it."

He is both angry and adamant, "Well, you'd better fucking believe it. Have you ever known me to be wrong about something so important? If you didn't spend so much time catting around in Miami on long weekends, you might know what's going on. In your absence, your husband has been talking to his lawyers. No doubt drawing up divorce papers. And if the goddam divorce goes through, there will be no inheritance."

Savannah Lindstrom, alias Anna Alcot Jennings, decides acquiescence is now her best bet.

Russell goes on, "Tomorrow is Thursday. Dave Richards tells me you leave for Miami every Friday. That's when Jennings brings in his legal team. Tomorrow night is our last chance before they meet again over the weekend. Time is of the essence. We have to finish him off before you can be served with divorce papers. Now listen carefully and take notes. Don't make me repeat myself."

Savannah now knows she badly miscalculated her hold on Preston. She admonishes herself, *Shouldn't have gotten so bored. Could have been more patient. Should have spent more time with your husband, his daughter and granddaughter. Instead of in Miami.*

She ponders, *Shoulda, coulda, woulda. Water under the bridge. Better listen and do what he says before it's too late.*

Russell outlines his scenario for tomorrow, Thursday night. He asks her for the time the perimeter house lights will go off. That's when he'll scale a wall, deliberately leaving the trail of a burglar. He'll enter the mansion through a window she designates. Once inside, she'll show him where her jewelry is kept and where Jennings sleeps. He'll kill the old bastard and take the jewelry. She will set off the alarm after the fact. It will appear to be a robbery that Preston, unfortunately, interrupted.

He tells her with Jenning's death there can be no divorce. Then, with his legal acumen and resources, he'll make sure she gets a big share of the inheritance.

At least, that's what he would have his partner in crime believe. In describing his revised plan to her, Underwood held back something that was entirely vital to his scheme.

And to Savannah's life.

CHAPTER 57

Basic black is the designated fashion color for this evening. Russell wears a black jump suit, black cap, black sneakers and a face blackened with stage makeup. The makeup will come off once he's inside the mansion. He wants Preston to see who is ending his life.

It's 11:55 p.m., Thursday, November 5th, 1970. Russell waits in the dark outside the north wall of Presthaven. At 1 a.m. Friday morning, only the front gate will be lit and perimeter house lights will have gone off. That's when he will scale the wall, negotiate the grounds and reach a window Savannah has left open on the north side of the mansion.

At 1:15 a.m., The lights are still on and Russell wonders if Savannah has screwed-up again. Just then, the house lights do go off. He tosses a Ninja grappling hook over the twelve foot high north wall and pulls himself up via the attached rope. He leaves the hook and rope where it is, to be found as evidence of a robbery attempt. He then crosses an open stretch of lawn where he can no longer be seen from the gate house.

Crouching behind some shrubbery, he checks his weapons. Attaches a silencer to the barrel of a .38 Special. It will suppress both muzzle flash and noise. He also carries a .22 magnum light weight pistol strapped to an ankle, just in case.

His watch now says 1:40. He makes his way across a half mile of lawns and hedges. Then through some Royal Palms and Banyan Trees that surround the long driveway as it leads to the front porch. Veering off to the north end of the mansion, he spots the single, dimly-lit stained glass window to which he was directed by Savannah. In all, he's covered a serpentine mile and a half from the north wall to his destination.

At 2 a.m., he enters through the window of a sitting room where Savannah awaits. This was Betsy and Preston's favorite place in a very large house, where they shared a drink and a chat when he came home from work. It's where Betsy first told Preston that daughter Abbey was made pregnant by none other than the Russell Underwood who, ironically, has just returned.

Savannah half-whispers, "He's in his study down the hall. Sleeping off a bottle of Cutty Sark, his favorite bedtime beverage."

Russell says softly, "Hope the bastard's not too drunk to recognize me when I kill him."

*   *   *

Dawn is just coming up in the Everglades. Swamp life is stirring and it's getting hotter and more humid by the minute.

It has been a sleepless night for Cassie, Tony and especially Gibby, whose wounded head is still pounding. But when the heroic retired cop considers the alternative, he has no complaints.

As soon as it was light enough to see, Tony climbed down from the stilt house to hide the bodies of the albino brothers and retrieve their rifles. He also found his Glock from inside the shack where one of the bogus cops stashed it. That means they now have pretty good fire power. Four weapons in all, including Gibson's service revolver. Whenever Carmine and more of his men arrive through the marshes, they'll have the advantage of high ground. By 6 a.m., they are dead tired. But adrenalin has them ready and waiting for a reckoning.

Cassie's mind wanders to her twelve year old son. *PJ must be wondering where his mom and dad are. So far, life has been such a scary adventure for him. I pray that after today we can find some normalcy. At least I know he's safe with Juanita. She's probably giving him breakfast right now and then will be driving him to school.*

Juanita is Manny Delgado's daughter who works as a waitress at DolceAmore. She loves PJ and takes care of him when she and Tony are away. PJ now attends a private school for gifted children in North Naples, to which he has qualified with a high IQ. He's in the eighth grade already, but his exceptional intelligence has not affected his winning ways. He's the most popular kid in school and his mom is so very proud of him.

Right now, she misses her boy a lot. Remorseful and sick of the whole alias charade, Cassie can't help saying aloud what she's thinking.

"We're here right now in this God awful place 'cause of that million dollars. Look at all the misery it's caused. Poor, dear Lucas murdered. Harry McIntyre, too. PJ kidnapped. And you Gibby, wounded now. Even all those bad guys who were killed by Tony and you already. No doubt, more to come. When's it all gonna stop?"

She looks at Tony, "I have to say it, darlin'... I wish you'd never wired me that money."

Tony's eyes meet hers. Puzzled, he says, "I gave Lucas ten thousand to tide you over. But baby, I never wired you no million dollars."

CHAPTER 58

By September, 1984, Tony and Cassie had been back together for over a year. In all that time, they'd never discussed the origin of the million dollar deposit. Each assumed the other knew where it came from. Tony reasoned it was sent by her tycoon grandfather. Cassie was sure it was from Tony.

They regarded the money as a big nest egg. It would stay in her savings account at Bank of America until needed. Right now, the DolceAmore was doing well. But in the restaurant business, you never knew for how long. So Cassie toned-down Tony's life style. She got him out of the elaborate house he was leasing and into a more sensible place out of Port Royal and onto Gulf Shore Drive. Up to just a few minutes ago, the subject of how the million dollars got to her was never discussed. There was no need. They both thought they already knew.

But if it wasn't wired from Switzerland by Tony, then by whom? She was twenty one years old when she got it and granddaddy Preston died when she was ten. Harry McIntyre looked into his will and said it didn't come from there. Nothing made sense.

From Tony's point of view, it was pure keystone cops. Carmine thought the big deposit in Cassie's First Federal account was Mafia money, scammed by Tony. The million plus was scammed alright, but it wasn't in Cassie's bank. Tony blew it all in Florida and Italy. At least in Italy, the money was used to make more money. And that was invested, along with Manny Delgado's half interest, in a partnership that created DolceAmore.

Up to now, both Cassie and Tony are still living under false identities to hide from the Mafia. She as Elizabeth Harrison. He as Frank LaForge. They were hoping that a police trap at the cemetery would make the aliases unnecessary. Ex-detective Gibson hoped right along with them. But the police were outmaneuvered by Carmine Battaglia.

And so, here they are, sitting with guns ready in a decrepit old stilt house somewhere in the Everglades. At seven in the morning, the temperature is already nudging ninety-eight and air conditioning in a place like this is just a faraway fantasy. There is only a tired old generator to support a single ceiling fan and flickering lights. So they wait in hot, humid discomfort, with very little sleep, for yet another deadly encounter.

At least their fates will soon be resolved. Carmine and his men were closing in on them right now. It was either kill or be killed.

* * *

There was a similar situation taking place back in the year 1970. Killers were also closing in on their prey. This time, the target was Preston Dylan Jennings.

Russell, wiping off his blackface, quietly follows Savannah into the study. The room's only light source is a floor lamp by the big, red leather chair that now contains Preston. The eighty year old patriarch is snoring with his head back and an open book on his lap. An empty glass and a bottle of Cutty Sark sit on a table at his side.

Savannah stands by the door wondering what in hell Russell is up to now. She watches him walk quietly to Preston's desk, sit behind it and switch on the desk light. At that point she realizes what he's doing. He needs assurance that when the old man awakens, he'll know who is pointing that gun at him. But it's a mistake, because the light is also shining in Russell's eyes

Call it a sixth sense. Or perhaps he was tipped by the flash of new light. Preston awakens with half-closed lids. Through shuttered eyes, he can see Russell Underwood's well-lit face and the revolver aimed at him. He starts quickly thinking his way through the cobwebs... *Do not open your eyes. Let him think you're still asleep. He's here to exact revenge.*

He wants to talk or he'd have shot you already.

Russell's own eyes are still adjusting to the light trained on his face. In the next moment, Preston picks up the bottle of Cutty Sark at his elbow and flings it towards his adversary. From eight feet away, his target is easy to see and his aim is good. The whiskey bottle crashes against the side of Underwood's head and shards of glass bury themselves in his cheek.

Octogenarian or not, half-inebriated or not, Preston follows his throw with a lunge across the desk, grabbing his opponent by the throat. It sends Russell's gun rattling to the floor. As old as he is, it's now the ex-coal miner's kind of fight, and once again he's getting the best of it.

Savannah, from across the room, rushes for her partner's weapon on the floor. As she picks up the revolver, Preston is on top of Underwood and has him in a stranglehold. She pulls the trigger. There is a dull popping sound as a silenced bullet slams through Preston's back, fatally damaging his aorta.

Preston Dylan Jennings knows immediately that he's dying.

He looks at the picture of Betsy that has fallen off the desk and now lays aside his face on the floor. Taken over twenty years ago when she was sixty years old. She's smiling into the lens and at her husband who holds the camera. It was the last picture he ever took of her. And the last thing he'll ever see.

A very eventful life is now playing out like a fast newsreel in the theatre of Preston's mind... From dung boy in his old country to billionaire philanthropist in his new one... to the miracle Christmas present from Abigail and Jon Dornwell... Cassie Jean. His last prayer is that his legacy will serve her well.

Life leaves him with some fitting final thoughts, *Not such a bad way to go... in a drunken brawl that you were winning. And with Betsy right here beside you, as always, when you needed her.*

Be with you soon, my love.

CHAPTER 59

Russell Underwood picks himself up with a severely bruised throat. He's croaking like a frog and wondering, *How in hell did the old bastard beat you again? You're over twenty fucking years younger and had a gun on him! If it wasn't for your bitch partner, he'd have killed you.*

He owes his life to Savannah. But it changes nothing.

He holds out his hand for the gun. Still shaken from killing another husband, she places it in his palm. Another husband. Thanks to Russell, she got away with murder the first time. Again, thanks to Russell, this time will be very different.

He points the silenced revolver at her and grins. *True blackness cannot be seen. It's in the heart, mind and soul.* If an artist's definition of the color black is "the absence of light", then it will soon also define Savannah's life.

She looks at the face of her partner and tries to process what's happening, "Why are you pointing that thing at me? I just saved your goddam life."

Underwood responds, "And I once saved yours. But now you have murdered again and this time I'm not your lawyer. I'm your judge." His grin doesn't change, "Your avarice and stupidity have ruined a perfect plan and I'm sentencing you to death."

The beautiful murderess is totally bewildered. They say there's a fine line between genius and insanity. Has he crossed that line? Or is this some kind of colossal, sick joke? She says, "Have you forgotten that I shot Preston to save you? If I didn't kill him, you'd be dead. You killed his wife and God knows how many others. And you're judging me? Russell, you are in serious need of a fucking checkup from the neckup. "

He's always enjoyed her colorfully sardonic way of putting things. "I may be crazy darling, but I'm not stupid. And you just didn't get enough brains to go with all that beauty. You should have figured this one out for yourself... if Jennings was planning a divorce, he'd have had you investigated. So, you're already pegged as a fraudulent journalist. If I let you live, the cops will discover your true identity. And, let's face it, to lighten your sentence, you'd give me up in a Manhattan minute. But if you die with your husband at the hands of a burglar, they'll buy the murder of a rich man and his wife, even if she was a gold digger."

Savannah just stands there, dumbstruck. She should have thought all this through. Just like she should have with Ben Murcer's pre-op. Or with spending long weekends in Miami, ignoring Preston and his family. There's no denying, as a malevolent sociopath herself, the logic of a brilliant psychopath. A terrible look of resignation is now passing over her prepossessing features.

Still, Russell must admire the alluring face that catches the room's lamplight so perfectly. He now recalls a memorable scene from an old movie in which the star actress says, "I'm ready for my close-up, Mr. DeMille".

The actress standing before him also played a starring role... in his own theatrical production. But it was a bad performance and she failed, ruining the master plan he'd worked on for years. Now there are no parting lines for her to say. What's more, her own cold heart understands. They are two of a kind. Evil begets evil.

Russell puts his fingers to his lips and extends a pantomimed kiss to Savannah. He pulls the trigger and a beautiful face goes suddenly blank. It's her final curtain.

Fade to black.

*   *   *

Four weeks later, Russell Underwood is met at Presthaven by Security Chief Dave Richards. This time, he has arrived undisguised for a "business" meeting with Abigail Jennings Dornwell.

His paid observer chats with him at the gate house entrance, "I got you the appointment Mr. Underwood, but still don't feel right not giving her your real name."

"I told you Dave, with a Tallahassee law practice, it puts me at a disadvantage down here. I just want her to think of me as a local lawyer."

Richards says, "Well boss, go easy on her. She's been treated for depression in the past and with the murders last month, she's right on the edge of a breakdown. The security screw-up that night could easily get me canned."

Russell reassures him, "Don't worry. If this deal I'm bringing her goes through, I'll make sure you keep your job with a bigger salary and a bonus to boot."

"Well then, let's hope you get the deal done. But still, use discretion. She's vulnerable."

The confident attorney thinks, *Vulnerable is just the way you want her. And on the edge. All ready to be pushed off.* He gives Dave a reassuring nod, "Don't worry my friend, I'll take care of her." That's a promise he can keep.

Dave nods back, "Follow the road about a half mile to the circular drive. One of my men will be waiting on the front porch. He'll take you to old man Jennings' study. Mrs. Dornwell will meet you there."

Russell smiles inwardly, *What perfect symmetry. Your reunion with the former Mrs. Underwood will take place at the scene of her father's death. She couldn't have picked a better place to meet. And to say goodbye to dear old Presthaven.*

CHAPTER 60

"I could be at the Trump in Atlantic City right now, shootin' craps. But all of a sudden, I get dis phone call from da boss. 'Come to Florida', he says. Gimme a hand. I figure the sunshine state, not bad duty. So here I am, sharin' the misery in dis fuckin' mosquita infested shit hole."

Rocco Fornessa is unhappy. Likewise, another of Carmine's top Mafia soldiers, Charlie "Mad Dog" Santori. They've been spraying each other with "Off" bug repellent.

Santori says, "Or if it's gotta be Florida, what's wrong with Miami? Why the fuck here?"

Carmine, also in a bad mood, reponds. "Quit your bitchin' stupidos. Think aboudit. What better place to work people over and then get ridda the bodies? Would you wanna be in some crowded tourist place, or in a jungle? Good thing I don't pay you pazzos for your brains."

"Swamp Boy" Billy is taking it all in. He enjoys the strange accents along with the exchange of insults from his passengers as he steers the propeller-driven airboat through some swirling, muddy waters of Lake Okeechobee. This is the fastest way from Belle Glade where the mobsters boarded, to the old stilt house where they want to go. Billy is another good ol' cracker who works on occasion with the wiseguys from up north. He's a transplanted Cajun out of the Louisiana swamplands and is available to do almost anything for a buck.

For the past thirty minutes, Carmine has been trying to reach the shack to advise them of his arrival. He finally lets out a yell of frustration. "No answer. These fucked-up cellular phones. Half the time they don't work."

Rocco adds; "Yeah, and the other half, they ain't safe. I read about it. They let out some kinda stugats microwaves. Fuck 'em, who needs 'em!"

Billy suppresses a laugh. These guys may be killers but at least they're funny killers. He keeps himself amused by pointing out two alligators sunning by the shoreline. He knows it will provoke an amusing reaction.

He gets one from Charlie, "I hate them ancient ugly mudafuckahs. Dey shoulda disappeared wit da dinosaurs two million fuckin' years ago."

Swamp Boy can't hold it in any longer. He laughs out loud.

Meanwhile, Carmine Battaglia pays no attention to the chatter. He's reminiscing and pondering, *How the fuck did it come to this? You had it going so good. Avoided all those Rico convictions. Got the fattest jacket in the Jersey D.A.'s office and they still can't lay a finger on you. Over and over, you proved you got the brains and the cajones. But then that fucking Vince Vega has to get into your life. Scams from la famiglia. Takes down two of your best guys at that garage. This is one vendetta that won't end until the prick is "morto nella tomba".* (Dead in the grave.)

The airboat has been on the water for almost an hour. Somebody once said that getting there was half the fun. But the fun is now over.

Shortly after they reach the last of the lake's tributaries, Billy stands out of his seat in front of the rear propeller cage. He gestures towards a flimsy looking structure on wooden stilts, less than a mile ahead. "That thar's the place, fellers."

CHAPTER 61

Cassie is the first to hear the airboat, then Tony. Gibby, down to one ear and with a head tightly bandaged, hears very little. But he can see.

Carmine is not arriving from the west through the mangroves as expected. Rather, by water from the other side of the stilt house. Tony thinks, *It figures. He'd be warned off getting here the hard way, like Cassie, Gibby and you were forced to. Too bad. The damned sawgrass would have slowed him down and cut him up.*

The arrivals are now close enough to be counted from the stilt house. Four of them, including what looks like a local guide piloting the boat.

Gibson takes charge of new tactics. A year ago at his insistence, Cassie took lessons in the use of a hand gun. He knew that a situation could arrive where she might have to defend herself. However, her target practice never included firing a rifle. There's no way she could shoot with accuracy from this distance. But hopefully, he and Tony would be capable. Their visitors are now about forty yards away.

He instructs Tony, "Wait for the bastards to leave the boat while the pilot ties up. Look for that open place on the trail as it turns directly towards us. Only room for single file, so I'll take the first guy, you take the second. Don't forget, we got bolt single action, so you need to lever and you get only one shot. While you take yours, I'll be reloading for number three."

Swamp Boy Billy steers his craft to a tiny dock in an area of the mangroves with firmer footing, sending two alligators scuttling away. He points to the trail that leads to the shack and ties the boat down as his

171

three passengers disembark.

Carmine follows his men along the trail. His mind is turning, *We should be getting a signal from them up in that shack by now*. Just as the trail turns towards the stilt house, he hears a sharp CRACK followed quickly by another CRACK. Rocco Fornessa goes down first, hit by Gibby's levered shot, mid chest. Charlie Santori is luckier. Tony's aim was not as good. Santori hits the ground with an exploding knee.

Carmine yells. "What the fuck?!! They're shooting at us from up there." He turns and runs back to where the airboat is tethered.

But Billy has heard the shots too. He knows somebody's firing at them. He quickly un-tethers while talking to himself, *Shee-it man. These fuckin' Mafias are at war. And I ain't hangin' around to see who wins*. He guns the motor, rotates the prop and blows out of there like he was in a boat race.

Carmine watches him go and panics. A rush of thoughts, *The Cajun sonofabitch took off. How the hell you ever supposed to find your way out of here? My guys are down. They still alive? Who's taking the pot-shots? Gotta stay low in the marshes and off the trail. Can't give whoever's up there any more target practice.*

He hears nothing from Rocco and assumes he's dead. But he's listening to Charlie groaning in pain, "Where you hit, Mad Dog?"

Santori answers from up ahead on the trail, "The leg. Shit, they blew out my fuckin' knee."

"Can you move?"

"I can crawl. That's it."

Carmine fights to keep it together, "We gotta get outta here somehow. Start crawlin' towards my voice. I'll give you a hand."

Charlie Santori, who was in line to move up in the chain of command to Atlantic City underboss, has much to live for. He crawls desperatly away.

But even flat on the ground, he's still in the open trail area and can be seen from above. Another shot rings out. Gibby has reloaded and levered. He hits his target in the lower back, severing the spine and ending a misbegotten life.

Above in the shack, Tony rushes for the door.

Cassie yells out, "Where are you going? Please Tony, don't go down there."

As Tony scrambles down the stilt house steps, he shouts back, "Carmine is still alive. If we're ever gonna be safe, I gotta get him." He heads for the mangrove, Glock in hand.

"He's right, darlin." Gibby says. He also moves to the steps. "We can't afford to let him get away. Stay put, I'm gonna follow Tony."

Battaglia hears someone coming. He has fallen back into the marshes near the edge of the mangrove where Billy untied the boat and sped off. He is on his stomach in thick, mucky vegetation. It's a stinking mess in there but he now has a clear shot at anyone coming after him on the trail.

Tony reaches the open part of the trail and the body of Rocco. He then moves to the spot where Santori also lies dead.

Carmine can see him now. His mind races. *It's Vega. You finally got the prick.* He lays flat, resting on elbows. Steadies his aim, left hand supporting right, preparing to fire his Baretta.

As the Mafia kingpin savors revenge, he takes no notice of the primitive beast behind him. On full alert, it's cold eyes are trained on human prey.

Carmine feels a sudden, violent jolt. It's accompanied by spasmodic, muscular twitches. A weird sense of being ripped apart is accompanied by intense pain that shoots through his lower body. He turns, head over shoulder, to a paralyzing sight. There is a bloody, severed leg in the jaws of an alligator.

At first, it doesn't dawn on him that it's his. But when realization hits, it hits like a semi. Carmine's horrified eyes bulge along with a throat that is swallowing his screams.

Tony inches forward. Just in time to see a second, larger gator dragging away the rest of the Cosa Nostra Capo. The prehistoric monster slithers off to water's edge with its capture.

For Tony it's a numbing sight, filled with mixed emotions of intense dismay and relief. A horribly bizarre thought crosses his mind, *The man was a bit of a reptile himself. Now he's gone for good... joining distant relatives.*

Gibby, who has just caught up, asks, "What happened?"

Tony doesn't want to think about it, let alone describe it. He can only manage, "Carmine got carried away and went for a swim. Arrivederci."

An hour later, Swamp Boy Billy returns, along with a second airboat and the police. Cassie, Gibby and Tony are escorted out of the Everglades. The nightmare is over.

CHAPTER 62

Russell Underwood sits in Preston Dylan Jennings' big, red leather chair awaiting the arrival of his former wife, Abigail Jennings Dornwell. He now regards the chair as his throne. The king is dead. Long live the king.

The funeral was worthy of royalty, alright. Russell was there, along with hundreds of others. It was pomp and circumstance befitting a billionaire philanthropist. It's rumored that he's bestowed hundreds of millions to charity.

The funeral itself was enough for the attorney/serial killer. He chose not to attend church services or any of the tributes. Instead, he had another, more important appointment. It was with Ralph Gorda, the young paralegal from Carter, Togias and Hill. Russell required some additional, valuable information. Ralph was made a "Mafia Offer", one he couldn't refuse.

This one went well beyond the five thousand he got for the name of The Crothers Group. Russell put a huge incentive on the table. Gorda could jump-start his career as a junior associate in the very successful law firm of Underwood and Associates. He would be paid a starting salary of $80,000 per year. In addition, he'd receive a $100,000 bonus upon delivery of the information Russell sought.

All things considered, a cheap price to pay for the last will and testament of Preston Dylan Jennings.

Once again, Gorda was an ideal choice. He'd been in on the drafting of Preston's will from the beginning. He was familiar with its nuances as well as where the documents were kept. His task was to leave with them in his briefcase after work Friday night, deliver them to Russell and collect his bonus. Whereupon, over the weekend, Russell would make a number of critical changes. The documents would then be returned via Ralph on Monday morning.

The changes did not affect Preston's charitable donations. That part of the will was already set in cement. But he was still in the process of eliminating a fraudulent wife from his will and drawing up divorce papers. So the changes that involved family bequeaths were not yet completed, and therefore unsigned.

Russell's timing was both good and lucky. Changes were made with a minimum of difficulty and Preston's signature was easy to forge. But there were two others in the law firm of Carter, Togias and Hill who were privy to the drafting of the will. They could raise doubts about his revisions.

That's where he got lucky twice. Associate Marje Verty became pregnant and left the firm shortly after the early draft meetings. Then, Underwood arranged an "accident" for sixty-seven year old Senior Partner Jason Carter. The brakes on his Bentley failed. Fortunately for Jason, the crash wasn't fatal. Fortunately for Russell, Carter had been planning on retirement. Hospitalization made it immediate.

Attorney Underwood now had a safely revised version of the will and a contract he'd drawn up for his ex-wife to sign. They were in his briefcase and ready for review with Abigail.

Abbey is twenty minutes late for their appointment. Russell pretends he's unaware she has entered the study. He has his face buried in legal papers. Just as she sits at her father's desk, he lifts his head. Abbey immediately gets to her feet, "How on earth did you get in here? And why?"

Russell's eyes hold hers, "Sit down my dear, and I'll tell you why." What he tells her will change the lives of Abigail Jennings Dornwell and her daughter Cassie Jean forever.

CHAPTER 63

Her tenth birthday was one Cassie Jean Dornwell would never forget. And with good reason. For the first time, there was no party. And no Presthaven, either.

That unfortunate fact was decided in her grandfather Preston's study when her mom met with Russell Underwood. Abbey thought later, she should have simply walked out of the room as soon as she saw him. But curiosity triumphed over common sense. She was once again eighteen years old, mesmerized by his self-assured presence. Why has he now returned to her home?

Her former husband is determined it will not be her home for long. Reposed in her father's chair, he looks as if he already owns the place. She sits behind Preston's desk, arms crossed, hands hugging her shoulders as if to ward off the shivers to come.

Russell starts vindictively, "You let you father destroy our marriage. You never made a single effort to come to me after he threw me out."

Abbey's response includes a question, "And why would I come to you... for more beatings? Russell, my father did not destroy our marriage. You did."

"No, no. We might have been able to work things out, but you never made an attempt. Not even a phone call. I don't like to be ignored. Such behavior comes at a price."

He is now deadly serious, "Let me explain about 'price'. Everything does have one. Especially good information. Like the kind I got from your father's will. The kind that said a company I have since come to own, would be the beneficiary of Presthaven. But only with your permission, of course. Before I leave, my dear, I shall have that in writing."

Abbey straightens in her chair, "Don't be so sure of yourself. I'll never leave here. Not as long as I continue to live in Florida."

Russell leans back, lighting a Marlboro. "Oh, I don't insist you leave Florida at all. Just Presthaven. This time of year, the climate in Florida is too nice. The climate of corruption, as well. If you're smart enough to manipulate the law in this state, you can achieve anything." He takes a long drag on his cigarette. "I've accomplished that. Your father's will has been rewritten. It specifically states that all previous wills are revoked and he was of sound mind when he signed this last one." He waves it in front of her her, "You and your daughter are no longer in it. But I am."

Abbey's hands tighten on her shoulders, "Why are you telling me all this? I'll go to my my lawyers. I'll go to the police. And you'll go to jail when I prove fraud."

The brilliant attorney is no longer responding. But the psychopathic serial killer is, "You won't go anywhere to see anyone, my dear. Because, you see, I'm the one who murdered both your mother and father." He smirks, "Hell, I even got rid of that 'wicked stepmother' of yours. Another killing or two means nothing to me."

Her hands can no longer control the trembling. Distraught eyes are brimming over. Russell knows it's time to push his already fragile ex-wife over the edge.

Therefore, he's saved his best for last, "If you breathe a single word of what I've just told you to anyone, your child will be my next victim."

Abigail fights harder for composure than at any time in her life, *You can either fall apart or keep it together for Cassie. Somehow you have to survive this. The man is psychotic. But he's always been brilliant; way too smart for you. If you make him want to kill Cassie, HE WILL.*

Her stunned silence is a positive for Russell. From the time he first met her in college, she was an open book.

"I know your daughter's birthday falls on Christmas. Tell her there'll be no party this year. I want you both out of here by then."

Underwood takes the papers requiring her signatures out of his briefcase and places them on the desk. Abbey just stares at them, numb to the bottom of her being.

He stands over her and says, "After you leave Presthaven, you'll be under close scrutiny. The people on my payroll are very watchful, very thorough. Remember, no lawyers, no police, nobody at all is to know what's transpired here."

He points to signature lines on the documents that would transfer Presthaven to his newly acquired company, The Crothers Group, LLC. His instruction is direct and matter of fact, "Now, you will sign where indicated. And if you mention anything about what I've told you, your daughter will die."

Abbey was caught in a tight, frightening net that denied her calm reasoning. But there was one reason she couldn't deny. Her daughter's life.

So she signed.

CHAPTER 64

Banishment from Presthaven made a new woman of Abigail Jennings Dornwell. Amazingly, after she was forced out of that privileged, cloistered environment, she was feeling a lot better about herself.

The care and protection of Cassie gave her the motivation she had lacked for years. She could no longer sit around and do nothing... getting treated for depression, feeling sorry for herself. So Abbey went job hunting. She landed her first job as a swtchboard operator at a successful Florida-based company called Minute Maid. She then moved into receptionist and secretarial positions at Kelly Girl Services in Zellwood and office Manager at the Bolton Ford dealership in Orlando.

Early on, Cassie's nanny Gussie had lost her husband Willie to cancer and was also dismissed by Russell. She reunited with Abigail and Cassie. That was a blessing, enabling Abbey to pursue better jobs while Gussie shopped, cooked and cared for her daughter.

The first three years on their own were spent largely in a variety of efficiency apartments, six to eight months at a time. There were also changes of schools, but thanks to her previous home-tutoring, Cassie maintained a B grade average.

But Preston's "life Lessons" were the ones she valued most. He once told her "Nobody can teach you who you are. That's something you must learn for yourself." She was determined to become someone who would make her granddaddy, her momma and Gussie proud.

After leaving Presthaven, Abbey insisted that Cassie wear her father Jon's St. Christopher medal. Cassie knew it was important or her mother would never have parted with it. Beyond the medal, Gussie was her guardian, accompanying her on the long walk to and from school. On weekends, the family of three would go to the movies that Cassie loved so much. Or they'd picnic and swim in Apopka's Dream Lake.

Cassie was happy with her mom and Gussie, but all the moving around made it difficult for her to maintain childhood friendships. It was something she always missed. She also missed not knowing why they had to leave Presthaven to begin with. Abbey would never tell her.

Walking and bicycling were their main modes of transportation until Abbey was able to afford a used car. She had created a decent life for Cassie, Gussie and herself, and was proud of her new found independence and accomplishment.

But she continued to live in the threatening shadow of Russell Underwood. Feeling his eyes were always on her, she had totally abided by his secrecy edict. Nevertheless, she sought retribution for the murders of her parents and the injustices suffered by her family. Surely, Russell would someday pay for those horrible crimes. Surely the falsified will could be overturned. Abbey waited patiently for an opportune time to go to the authorities for justice, without endangering her daughter's life.

She and her little family had more than survived their first three years away. They were now living permanently in a better apartment and were celebrating Christmas, as well as Cassie's fourteenth birthday. But the next year would change everything.

* * *

While Abbey was struggling, Russell was enjoying the place once called Presthaven. By then, he'd re-christened it with an elaborate bronze plaque that simply said "Underwood Private Property". There was some difficulty with ridding himself of The Crothers Group, but the law suit with Malcolm Crothers was settled out of court ten months after he took possession. He now had sole ownership of the grand estate. He lived there alone, retaining only Richards and his security people, while hiring a new staff of household servants and groundskeepers. He established a business branch in nearby Orlando as an adjunct to his law offices in

Tallahassee, and split work time between the two. It was over four years since he threw out his ex-wife, her daughter and the black nanny who had since rejoined them. He knew of that occurence and everything else in Abigail's life. He was kept well-informed by the people he'd hired to keep her on a leash.

Russell, now in his fifties, had always been totally successful in hiding his secret life. His serial kills now totaled thirteen and the brilliant psychopath was more self-assured than ever. There was no doubt in his mind that he could continue undetected through any homicide investigation.

His twisted mind still resented the fact that it was Savannah and not he, who killed Preston. It had now been four years since he murdered her. More than enough time to wait for another termination.

That maniacal, obsessive-compulsive urge to rape and kill was on him again.

CHAPTER 65

During her third year of exile from Presthaven, Abigail made a good friend in Florence Wallace. Florence proved to be an even better friend by landing her a job as secretarial assistant to the manager of Bolton Ford, a successful auto dealership in Orlando.

Flo Wallace was the star saleswoman at Bolton. A convivial, plumpish peroxide blonde in her mid fifties, she had a way of charming many customers into buying cars. Everyone seemed to enjoy her humorous repartee. Sometimes the laughter could be heard all the way from the showroom to Abbey's back office.

The cutesy motto on Florence's business card was *"Go with the Flo"*. Abbey, in the interest of both friendship and self-improvement, did just that. The obliging Flo helped her not only at work but often at home.

A divorcee with time on her hands, she pitched in on days off, helping Abbey and Gussie with getting Cassie to and from school. And it was Flo who got Abbey a steal on a used car, using her influence with their boss. She became a trusted friend in whom Abbey felt she could confide. For years, in fear for Cassie's life, she'd been unable to share her deadly secrets. But now there was someone who might help.

In Abbey's mind, the stealing of her home was by far the lesser of the evils done by Russell. She was doing well enough on her own, and was confident she would someday win back Presthaven. But she was resolved that the murder of her parents could no longer go unpunished.

So she'd share her secrets with her friend. Flo would advise her and assist in getting needed information to the police and her former attorneys.

After all, she was not only someone who had proven her friendship, she was a successful woman and very smart.

She had to be. She worked for Russell Underwood.

*   *   *

Another well-paid observer had paid off well.

Underwood listened with interest as he was told about Abbey being ready to go to the law. Florence Wallace, unlike Security Chief David Richards, didn't give a damn about Abigail, Cassie or Gussie. She was in reality not a jovial good samaritan, but a bitter, vindictive woman.

Despite her success in business, she hated both her former husband and her current life. Like Russell, she wore the mask of sociability well. What she now lived so deceptively for was enough money to spend the rest of her time in France. Underwood had paid handsomely for her sleuthing. And his next assignment would cover the remainder of what she required for a comfortable retirement.

Russell laughed inwardly, *You do have a way with motivating some innately sociopathic women.*

Actually, he no longer needed the prerequisite of Abbey disobeying his edict. The satanic evil deep inside him had already dictated another killing. The fact that his former wife was ready to challenge his authority just made it all the better. She'd lose her daughter for doing so. And that would torture her for the rest of her life. *The devil loves to play God.*

His plan was simple. On January 10th, 1972, Flo would pick up Cassie from high school and deliver her to him. His conspirator would then be given $200,000 in cash for her part in the kidnapping. She planned to depart immediately for Paris, not knowing, nor particularly caring, about what happened to a barely fourteen year old child.

But on the designated day, Florence Wallace made a mistake. She had alerted Gussie that she'd pickup Cassie at school, but forgot to tell Abbey, which she previously had never failed to do. A normally astute

184

mind was otherwise occupied with plans to catch a 5 p.m. Air France flight out of Orlando International.

When she saw Flo leave the showroom early, Abbey called Gussie. But Gussie was out shopping. Without confirmation, the always concerned mom had no way of knowing if Flo was simply leaving for the day or going to pick up Cassie. So Abbey had no choice but to leave early herself, and make the drive to pick up her daughter.

She arrived at District Five Orange County Public School late. But just in time to see Cassie climb into Flo's new, white Ford Fairlane. Relieved, she started to turn back. But noticed Flo's car headed in the opposite direction of home.

Curiosity made her follow. It was a twenty minute drive through the suburbs of Orlando. Just as they entered the Winter Park area, Abbey got caught at a light and watched helplessly as the Fairlane got smaller and smaller in the traffic ahead. It seemed like forever before the light changed. By that time she'd lost them.

Something compelled Abbey not to give up. She drove through four different neighborhoods of Winter Park, up and down, block after block. Now frustrated, she looked at her watch and realized she'd been searching for 45 minutes.

Then, out of nowhere, some great luck. In a more secluded, higher-end section with acre zoning and fewer homes, she finally saw the white Fairlane well down the road and moving directly towards her. It came from what looked like a big Tudor-style home sitting on a cul-de-sac. Abbey braked to wave it down, but it sped right by. She could however, clearly see Flo in the driver seat. Otherwise, the car was empty. Which begged the question, *Where the hell was Cassie?*

Abbey drove to the cul-de-sac and moved quickly up a long flagstone pathway to the front of the Tudor. At the bottom step up to an arched oak door, something shiny reflected in the late afternoon sun.

It caught her eye... a silver chain. On it, a St. Christopher medal.

CHAPTER 66

Abbey rang the doorbell with urgency and trepidation. When there was no reponse, she banged on solid oak with both fists.

Russell Underwood never heard the racket at the front door. He was upstairs preoccupied with a screaming, teenage tigress. Granddaddy Preston taught Cassie to never give up. She was doing her best. But this demon had already torn off her clothes and hurt her badly. He viciously, relentlessly, painfully, pounded into her body. Her odds were insurmountable: a two hundred pound man versus a ninety pound child.

As for the saving of her honor, that battle was already lost. She was now fighting for survival. She couldn't breathe through her nose, it was full of blood. The pain in her vagina was agonizing. Attempting to get out from under him, she called on what strength she had left and jammed the point of her knee into his groin.

He fell off her, doubling up in pain. This was only a fourteen year old girl, but no woman he'd ever attacked put up a better fight. To Russell's twisted mind, it only made the challenge and the conquest better. Like his other rapes, this was more about power than sex. His victim was kneeling on the bed now, looking for something, anything, with which to defend herself. But Cassie saw only her blood, seeping through sheets.

At that moment, Abbey went running around to the side of the house, looking for an open window, to no avail. Then she heard her daughter scream. She quickly found a rock the size of a football, and hurled it through a window.

After scrambling inside, she heard the ruckus from upstairs and searched for something to use as a weapon. In her panic, she could find nothing except the rock she'd just thrown. Grasping it in her hands, she took to the stairs, stumbling, heading in the direction of her daughter's screams.

The noise was coming from behind a bedroom door. When she threw it open, Russell, otherwise engaged, never noticed. He wore latex surgeon's gloves and his face was smeared with colorful Apache war paint, no doubt as a disguise, but also to terrorize. Still, Abbey recognized who it was. Her bastard of an ex-husband was sitting nude on Cassie's chest, his knees pinning down her arms, his hands around her throat. He is watching, mesmerized with morbid fascination as his victim's eyes grow dim while her larynx is being slowly crushed.

His maniacal intensity is such that Underwood doesn't know where the blow to his head comes from.

It topples him over, unconscious, from the bed to the floor.

Abbey yells out, "I should bash in your brains, you evil sonofabitch!" She immediately seizes her daughter's torn dress and puts it back on her.

"Get out of here honey, run fast. Go next door. Call the police".

Cassie, still badly shaken, says, "Momma, come with me. Let's both of us go!"

"No honey, I don't want this murderin' maniac to get away. I'm stayin' here." She holds up the rock, "If he comes to, I'll hit him again. Now, you do what I say and run, dammit. Run fast as you can. Get help!"

Cassie has never seen her mom so angry, distraught, determined. She rushes down the stairs and out the front door. She aches from top to bottom as she accidentally kicks away the medal she deliberately dropped for someone to find. The medal had served its purpose. Her only purpose now is to get to a neighbor for help.

Unfortunately, the neighbor was not home. Neither were two others. Cassie ran desperately and breathlessly across acres of lawns until she found an occupied house. The police are called, but by the time they get to the Tudor on the cul-de-sac, it is too late.

Russell had regained consciousness and tackled Abbey before she could raise the rock again. Cassie was just running next door when he was on her mom, choking the life out of her. Mercifully, it was over quickly. To Russell's anger. Things were not going at all according to plan. He wanted his ex-wife to agonize over her daughter's death. Since Abigail knew too much, he planned to kill her too. But tomorrow, not today. And not like this.

Her little bitch got away. And there would be no tomorrow for Abbey. His only choice was to kill her quickly. There was barely enough time to cover his tracks and get out of there. Things had gone all wrong. He'd just have to catch up with the girl later. For now, he had to settle for escaping detection once again.

*   *   *

When Florence Wallace debarked from Air France Flight 510 at Charles De Gaulle Airport, she headed straight for the baggage counter. A uniformed limo driver was waiting with a hand-lettered sign that had her name on it. She approached the tall, mustachioed Frenchman and identified herself. She was told there was a limousine waiting to take her to her downtown hotel, the Paris-Le Grande. Courtesy of a Mr. Russell Underwood.

Flo thought, *A nice touch. The man does have class. This will be a lot better than fighting through Parisian traffic with one of those crazy frog cab drivers.*

But it wasn't better at all. Because the limo driver was a professional assassin. He was enticed with a promise that his victim was carrying a significant amount of U.S. currency in the form of cash. It would be all his if he discreetly eliminated her.

So, Flo never does get to her hotel. In fact, Ms. Florence Wallace is never seen or heard from again. Russell had once more covered his tracks. Just as he did with the police investigation in Winter Park, Florida.

The only blood and fingerprints left at the rape and murder scene belonged to Abigail and Cassie. No substantial or usable forensic evidence was collected, including the residue of face paint and semen. The paint proved to be obscure and untraceable. And in 1972, DNA testing was not yet available.

Even more frustrating, after looking at countless mug shots and artist's sketches, Cassie could not make positive identification. Homicide's only remaining lead was the Tudor house used by the murderous rapist. But the owners were of no help. They were away in Europe when their home was leased through a broker for cash, under a false name. Thus, this case, like so many of Underwood's others, went cold.

The loss of a mother and a brutal rape was a devastation that would have emotionally crippled almost anyone. Somehow, some way, Cassie would eventually survive and be stronger for it. She took to heart what her granddaddy told her about learning, under duress, who she was.

But awake and in dreams, she carried the twin tragedies with her for the rest of her life. She had lost her mom to a mysterious stranger and was never told how her grandparents died. She didn't even know why she was banished from Presthaven. But sensed it in her bones. Somebody was out to get them all. She was part of a Jennings family curse.

Nine months later, with PJ's arrival, the curse turned into at least one blessing.

CHAPTER 67

She's in that bedroom again, struggling with a terrifying Apache warrior. She fights with all her strength, but she's losing. That awful woman Flo, she thought was such a good family friend, gave her to the Indian for lots of money. Oh, God, don't they know she's barely fourteen? Why is he hurting her down there? She's bleeding. Choking now. It's getting dark. Cassie is suddenly jolted by the touch of a hand.

Patting her shoulder, Tony says, "Honey, you're having another bad dream." He takes her gently into his arms.

It's 4 a.m. on August 20th, 1989. And it slowly dawns on thirty-one year old Cassie Jean Dornwell that she's in her own bedroom, not that other, all too familiar one from out of the past. She has no doubt the nightmare was because today will be PJ's seventeenth birthday.

*　　　　*　　　　*

She always thanked heaven for giving her son character to go with his intelligence. If brains came from an unknown father, fortunately none of the other maniacal traits followed along. PJ is now in his Freshman year at Yale on a full scholarship, studying law. He came home last night for a grand party planned for later today. His Asthma is long gone and he's now an athlete as well as a scholar. Eight years ago, Tony took him to his first game at Yankee Stadium. That hooked him on Baseball. Now he plays first base for the Yale varsity, a position once held by George H. W. Bush, who would soon have an even better position: forty-first President of the United States.

When she thought back to the raising of PJ, Cassie was reminded of something that had been so troubling in her own childhood. Momma Abigail never gave her the real reason for leaving the Presthaven she loved so dearly. Abbey of course, felt she had to protect Cassie from the truth.

Because her own mom kept the truth from her, she was determined to be honest with her son. If she was old enough at fourteen to get raped, her son was old enough at the same age to learn about it. PJ was smart and such a well-adjusted child that she felt he could be told the truth. And he was. His mother never knew his father. She was not a wife, but a victim.

Nevertheless, Cassie made sure he knew his birth was a true blessing for her. He was always loved as much as anyone could be. Very possibly because of that love, PJ had the maturity to accept and deal with the knowledge. But he was naturally curious about the identity of his biological father. And from the time he became aware of the violence put upon his mom, he was motivated to find out who that man was. PJ was only fourteen, but knew it was time to put childish things aside.

To this day, Cassie has no idea why she was banished from Presthaven. Or who raped her. Or who sent her that million dollars eight years ago. PJ has been working on those riddles since he was told about them. He's been on it for two years. And for the last twelve months, it's been "balls to the wall" as his college buddies would say. He's finally ready to give his mom all the answers.

*   *   *

As Tony turns over and goes back to sleep, Cassie moves into her usual curl. She no longer dreams, but does remember...

She cried for months after her momma saved her life and was then taken so cruelly from her. She thought Abigail's death was the sole reason for her sickness. It wasn't. Gussie, who was now taking care of her full time, deduced she was with child.

In 1972, rape was grounds for a legal abortion. A child herself, Cassie was naturally confused, frightened and overwhelmed. There was a life or death decision to be made. And only she could make it. She found her answer in her prayers and in her heart. Giving birth to this child was simply the right thing for her to do.

Gussie was midwife to the home birth. Cassie named her boy Preston Jon in honor of her granddaddy and daddy. She was barely more than a child herself when she became a mother. That meant she had to grow up in a hurry. She and Gussie made it through most of that first year on love, determination and money Abbey saved and kept at home under the mattress, instead of in a bank. Cassie quit school to care for her baby while Gussie got work cleaning houses to support them. They had to guard the secret of their little family carefully inorder to avoid scrutiny by Florida Health and Welfare. Otherwise, PJ would be placed under state care or in a foster home.

Late that second year, Cassie lost her dear nanny Gussie to lung cancer. Not yet eighteen years old, she was now alone with her child and bereft. A kindly, widowed neighbor named Lacey Dugan was living on a Florida Benefits Program that gave her access to food and medical assistance. She was a godsend, sharing her "wealth" with Cassie and baby sitting for PJ. Thanks to Lacey, the young mom could set out to find a job and get a new place to live.

*   *   *

She's still not sleeping, but the memories are getting better. In 1978, at age seventeen, she spots an ad in the Orlando News Classifieds and has an interview with Manny Delgado. He takes pity on her, overlooks the fake ID and gives her a bartender job at The Booby Trap. Her luck has changed. Shortly thereafter, she answers another ad and meets dear old Lucas Wilson, who leases her a little apartment over his garage.

Cassie finally drifts off to sleep. This time with her mouth turned up at the corners.

It's 1979 again. The year of Mariposa. They're in the county courthouse. Manny Delgado is best man and his wife Renee is maid of honor. PJ is the ring bearer and Lucas gives the bride away. Her marriage to Tony will always be one of the happiest days in her life. She did lose him for awhile, but won't let that come between her and a good dream. Because he's here now, sleeping right beside her.

CHAPTER 68

"Strummin' my six string... on my front porch swing...

Jimmy Buffett is not in Margaritaville searching for his lost shaker of salt. *Stepped on a pop-top... blew out my flip-flop...* He's right here on the back lawn for PJ's seventeenth birthday.

The famous exponent of bars, beaches and laid-back living is standing in an amped-up gazebo, playing guitar and singing his hits to the delight of partygoers. Just another Tony Roselli extravaganza. He had approached Buffett's manager with a generous fee for his man's personal appearance. Tony knew Cassie and PJ were big "Parrotheads", and nothing was too good for his wife and his son. The popular entertainer was playing a concert at nearby Naples Philharmonic Center. It would be a convenient gig, so he said, "Why the hell not?" and joined the party.

Mr. and Mrs. Roselli were doing very well with the DolceAmore name. They have added two new southwest Florida restaurants, one in Marco Island and one in Estero. And they still had that million dollar gift in their savings account. So there were sufficient funds to host a gala party with a celebrity guest and performer in their new Pelican Bay Colony home. Friends and neighbors, new and old, are celebrating. It's August in Florida and therefore, hot. Most are dressed in shorts, and all are having a good time. Among special guests are long-since retired Michael Gibson and his wife Adrienne, who are chatting with Manny and Renee Delgado.

Gibby looks Manny over and says, "First time I saw a Mexican without a taco in one hand and a Corona in the other."

Manny fakes anger and returns the assault, "I'm Cuban, you Mick bastard. How come it's after twelve noon and you're still sober?"

Tony, who is turning a roasting hog on his barbecue spit, is delighted to hear his old friends playing so well together.

After Jimmy Buffett finishes his inimitable "Cheeseburger in Paradise" he joins the three caballeros for a beer and some horseshoe throwing. Later, a hundred and ten guests partake in a good old fashioned southern feast put together by Cassie and the staff at DolceAmore. There is roast hog, southern fried chicken, corn on the cob, baked beans, collard greens, potato salad, corn bread and of course, cheese grits and shrimp. To say nothing of a large selection of wines, hard liquor and desserts.

After dessert, PJ goes ceremoniously through his birthday presents to much applause. Cassie then requests a final number from their world-famous entertainer. She introduces a song with her favorite funny title: "The weather is here. Wish you were beautiful." Buffett obligingly plays and sings the evening's finale, bringing the house down.

Tiki torches are flaming out and the party is over. Guests happily scatter in all directions. The Roselli's newest friend Jimmy is picked up in a rented limo. Among the last to leave are the benefactors Cassie can never thank enough. Manny and Gibby are given warm hugs and kisses by the party's hostess.

*   *   *

As the cleanup crew goes to work on a big, messy back lawn, Preston Jon hugs his mom and dad and thanks them for a memorable birthday party. And, of course, for so much more. They have all come a long way in a short time. After the Everglades and the demise of their Mafia enemies, Cassie and Tony were able to resume life with real names. Their restaurants were doing well. PJ was studying law, getting great grades. But writing was now his passion. Over the past four years, Roselli family life had finally become peaceful.

All was well. Except, of course, for those troubling questions out of Cassie's past. That's where PJ comes in. His youthful face turns serious as he ushers his parents to the back porch.

After they settle down, Tony says, "Okay pal, what gives?"

His son answers, "Four years ago, mom told me about some bad things that happened in her life. Riddles that still bothered her. They bothered me, too. When I was fourteen, I even wrote a little two-line poem about it." He takes out an old, crinkled sheet of paper and reads...

> *"The rest of us stand in a circle and suppose,*
> *While the riddle sits in the middle and knows."*

He goes on, "I had to get into the middle. To what mom calls the "Jennings Family Curse". For the past few years, on and off, I've been working my way in. Done a ton of research at Yale Library. Looked up the history of mom's family. Went through newspaper articles, medical records, psychiatric profiles, police rape and murder files, criminal trials... the whole nine yards, plus." He catches a breath and continues, "I went through everything, carefully, systematically. Even more than if I had to prepare a thesis or a dissertation for my Masters Degree. Through it all, I found one continuous thread... a common denominator, an overriding motive."

By now, Cassie and Tony know exactly where PJ is going. He has solved the riddles. He has answers to those questions that have haunted Cassie... Why was she exiled from Presthaven? Who raped her? Who sent her a million dollars?

Their son answers all three questions with a single name.

CHAPTER 69

In 1972, Russell Underwood was well aware that Abigail's daughter had given birth. Over the next few months, his spies kept him well-informed of Cassie's subsequent struggles.

So he had sired a son! He had no doubt the boy was his procreation. The one thing his selfish, misogynistic mind never anticipated was an heir to his fortune. Someone to mold in his image. This birth was a game changer.

Still, he had no use for an infant requiring child care. It was never his intention to take on that inconvenience. His son wouldn't be ready to mentor for years, anyway. Children were a nuisance and he disliked them almost as much as he did women. He had his doubts. Therefore, he'd wait at least five years to see if he wanted a son and an heir.

Russell loved to make complex plans and follow them to exacting execution. They usually involved murder. But this situation was quite different. He'd strategize carefully. If he decided to take his son, he'd get what he wanted. He always did.

*   *   *

Five years later, he was ready to adopt. On the eve of both Christmas and Cassie's twenty-first birthday in 1980, one million dollars was wired from The Bank of Switzerland to her own meager $25.50 account at First Federal. She came to the conclusion it was from Tony. Her only other guess was that somehow granddaddy Preston sent it, as Tony later presumed. She had asked a one-time friend, banker Harry McIntyre, if that was a possibility. Harry, before he became a Mafia victim, said his investigation of the will revealed that for some strange reason (of Russell's doing), no money was left to her mother or to her. And so, the gift from heaven remained a mystery.

Actually, it was a gift from hell. Because it came from Russell Underwood.

However, there was a problem with the deposit. The difficulty did not involve the money itself but rather a letter that was supposed to arrive with it. That letter was never seen by Cassie. Nor had Russell known she didn't get it. Therefore, the money's source remained a mystery to Cassie. There was an accident regarding that letter. Thanks to a distracted, about to retire bank manager named Charles Thompson, it was carelessly shredded along with a pile of expired confidential customer accounts and other useless paperwork.

*   *   *

Now, in 1989, multi-millionaire Russell Underwood is going through his desk files and finds a copy of that letter. He reads it with a degree of nostalgia.

Dear Ms. Dornwell,

Consider the accompanying one million dollars a good faith deposit as proof I am serious in regard to the following proposal.

I have been told you are a single mother in need of assistance.

You shall have it. I am prepared to pay you a sum that will make you a wealthy woman and provide you with comfort and security for the rest of your life.

You will receive this very generous payment upon your signed agreement to a transaction I wish to explain in person.

In the meantime, I prefer to remain anonymous.

Please call me collect at my private, secure number: 888 500 5000.

A friend.

Of course, the transaction Russell had in mind was the adoption of Preston Jon Dornwell, who was now the right age for mentoring. Kidnapping crossed his mind, and he supposed he could get away with it. He'd already proven so often that there were many terminally stupid people whose only occupational hope was Florida law enforcement or state government. But why chance it when a legal adoption can be made for money that, thanks to Preston Dylan Jennings, he can well afford.

The letter really wouldn't have mattered to Cassie except for the mystery of its origin. Even if she'd received it, such an offer would never have been considered. Underwood lived by the principle that everything had a price. He was used to either taking or buying whatever he sought. On the other hand, Cassie believed that some things were priceless, starting with her son.

But Russell had no way of knowing that. To his great annoyance and frustration, he never heard back from the girl he raped at age fourteen.

Once again, he put spies to work. They reported some bizarre activity had taken place after the money was received. First, she got married to a former Mafioso. Then there was a rogue cop who kidnapped the boy for a million dollar ransom. Then the Mafia got involved, thinking the money was stolen from them. People were killed in the process. After that, the girl, her son and the million disappeared (into Gibby's witness protection program).

For only the second time in his life, the brilliant attorney and serial killer had been seriously thwarted. First it was Jennings, who threw him out of Presthaven and forced Abigail into a divorce. Then it was the granddaughter who didn't acknowledge his offer, but kept his money and his progeny.

The Underwood psychosis lay dormant for quite some time. He thought it might be due to his advancing age. But now, he's getting that "kill itch" again.

For some reason, possibly shedding the Mafia threat, the granddaughter and her husband had resurfaced. And Preston Jon was out in the open, too. Yale University at age sixteen... more proof of a biological son.

In Russell's sick mind he was obliged to kill Cassie. He must make good on a promise to his ex-wife Abigail and to himself. He had to finish a job that only started with rape.

But his son was another matter. Does he kill his own flesh and blood, too? Or does he let him live as an heir? Shouldn't he carry on the name of Underwood? Will the son be a match for the father's cunning and intellect? Interesting questions.

He won't have to wait long for answers. PJ is on his way.

CHAPTER 70

The name Russell Underwood reverberates. Cassie's heard and read about the renowned attorney. But she was too heartbroken to ever revisit Presthaven. Therefore, she never saw the big bronze plaque by the front gates that read, "Underwood Private Property".

Thanks to her son, she now knows who acquired her granddaddy's estate, and how deviously and cruelly that was accomplished. She also now knows who raped her and where that million dollar windfall came from. When so many others for so many years could not, a driven PJ put it all together. She was sure he could accomplish just about anything he wanted.

And Preston Jon Dornwell wanted Russell Underwood. Real bad. As long as that monster lived, his mother was in mortal danger.

PJ is again methodically thinking it through, *He is a proven psychotic serial killer. But proven by whom? Only you, not the law. What you've been constructing for the past two years is the psychological profile of a brilliant madman. Even if your evidence is brought to light, it will take forever to get him convicted. In the meantime, he'll be free to do his thing. When he raped mom he meant to kill her, too. And would have if it weren't for her own mother. He may have lost track of her under Gibby's protection plan, but now she's out in the open again. And he'll be compelled to finish what he started.*

PJ comes to a reluctant but realistic conclusion, *No way can you go through a lengthy legal process. The law can't help you. You have to get him before he gets mom. Clearly, it's YOU who are now the law.*

After his birthday party, PJ does not return to the Yale campus in New Haven, Connecticut. He stays in Naples, Florida and fibs to his parents. Tells them he's working on an end-of-semester paper that he's better able to complete right here at home.

Then he works on a plan. Comes up with a beautifully simple one. He thinks, Do it like a blitzkrieg chess move. A direct frontal attack will catch him off guard. Walk right in and say "Hi, dad." Genius or not, it'll blow his deranged mind!

Of course, he'll need help to get into Presthaven.That's where Dave Richards comes in. That name kept coming up in PJ's investigations. He was hired to be Underwood's eyes and ears and thus became Security Chief at Presthaven. But from everything PJ could ascertain, the hired hand was not aware of his boss' true ulterior motives. Throughout the murder investigation of Preston and his second wife, he told the police that he suspected the wife might somehow be involved and could even have had an accomplice. PJ came to the conclusion that Underwood and his employee were not complicit, and thus contacted Richards.

They compared notes and facts, and were soon on the same page with their suspicions. In the process, their friendship was sealed when Richards was told that PJ's mom was none other than Cassie Jean, the pretty and polite little Shirley Temple look-alike he protected at Presthaven.

After that, came the clincher: PJ methodically went through detail after detail, year after year, offering proof that Dave's boss was not only a successful attorney, but also a psychotic serial killer. From that point on, the veteran lawman and the sixteen year old prodigy were dedicated to the common task of bringing down Russell Underwood.

They worked on their individual responsibilities for executing PJ's plan. Dave would build the box and have it positioned for their use. PJ would bring the accessories. They set the date. Time was of the essence, so the confrontation would come within two weeks of PJ's past birthday, on an evening in early September.

It's ten o'clock. The help has left. Russell Underwood finished his dinner thirty minutes ago and dismissed the servants. He has settled down with a fine French cognac, a Cuban cigar and his favored research literature, Krafft-Ebing's "Psychopathia Sexualis". The front gate phone rings and is picked up.

Dave Richards says, "Sir, can I see you for a minute?"

Annoyed, Russell responds, "You know I don't like interruptions in the evening. I hope it's important." When he's assured it is, "Come in then Dave, but make it fast."

As he opens the front door, someone standing behind Richards moves out into the light. Russell's brow furrows. It's like looking into a mirror out of the distant past.

For PJ, this is the best part. The part he's been waiting for, "Hi, dad."

For most of his life, Russell Underwood has enjoyed the expression on his victim's faces when they looked death in the eye. Now it's his turn.

PJ stares at his biological father. He sees himself in another fifty years or so. The three of them take seats in the ornately furnished living room. Their reluctant host offers them a cognac that is politely declined. He takes a slow, bravado puff on his cigar. There is a passing glance of annoyance towards Dave Richards.

PJ looks at the volume on Underwood's coffee table and says, "Why am I not surprised?"

Russell ignores the sarcasm and attempts cordiality, "I've been following your activities at Yale University, young man. Excellent grades. Good hitter on the baseball team. I was about ready to come visit you. You've saved me a trip to Naples."

PJ says, "I figured you might want to visit soon. That's why we're here. Were you coming by to say hello before or after you murdered my mother?"

That's a stopper. Unfortunately for him, Russell is nowhere near his new, lightweight Ruger pocket pistol. But why should he need a gun? He's in the comfort and safety of his own home, with his trusted security guard sitting next to him. An irony, indeed.

The celebrated, trial-tested attorney stays collected. "Why should I want to kill your mother, or anyone else?"

Dave Richards will answer that one, "Because you are a crazy fucking psycho, that's why."

PJ takes a small tape recorder out of his pocket, "We'd like your confession. We don't need everybody you've killed. Just those in the Jennings family will do for now."

Underwood scoffs and turns a witty phrase, "I'd like to take you seriously, but I don't want to insult your intelligence."

PJ responds, "They say confession is good for the soul. But since you don't have one, I guess it won't help, anyway."

Richards unholsters his Smith & Wesson.

Russell keeps his cool, "And what do you suppose you're going to do with that?"

"Whatever he wants." Says PJ, "And for now, he wants to take a walk with you and me."

CHAPTER 71

Underwood is escorted by Richards and PJ to the rear of his estate. They walk in silence with Russell's keen, frenzied mind racing.

It's a long walk, so he has plenty of time to think. No way to physically resist a burly security chief and a strapping seventeen year old. The best he can do under the circumstances, is barter and bribe. He offers them untold wealth if they will just let him live.

PJ says, "Your money's no good here. For once, you can't buy or steal something you want. And you're in no position to make deals. Anymore than you can ever kill anyone again." He now pauses to let what he's about to say sink in. "But we do intend to let you live. And for as long as you may want."

Russell's too wise and cynical to get his hopes up. His son is speaking in riddles. He conjectures, *They want to kill you. That's a given. But as long as you yourself can decide when, there's always a chance.*

Actually, there is no chance. PJ has planned a fittingly inevitable end to a horrible human being. Underwood deserves no mercy. Nor even a fast death. And he'll have neither.

They've now reached their destination on a back acre of the estate. Awaiting them is a four foot deep pit resembling a well with corners. There is also a thirty-six inch square solid hardwood box. Russell is smart enough to put it together quickly.

It's your coffin. They're going to bury you alive!

At first, his mouth opens in a silent scream. Then he kneels and finds the words... "No, no. Please. Not this way. Don't do this. Christ, have mercy.

Dave Richards says, "You satanic prick. You have the nerve to beg for mercy invoking the name of Jesus?"

He grabs a struggling Russell in a headlock, lifts him up and sets him into the box feet first. The whining, blubbering psychopath is then forced into a tight sitting position, knees to chin. Richards slams down a hinged, two inch thick wooden lid and locks it.

Underwood is now literally under wood, interred in a cramped tomb that will be his final resting place.

Besides Russell, the box contains water, food rations and a knife he can use on himself at a time of his choosing. PJ fits a breathing tube into a hole in the lid, and the square coffin is lowered into his grievous sire's grave.

Muffled screams can barely be heard on the way down. The pit is filled in with dirt. Only the breathing tube is left above ground. It will soon be rendered invisible as weed sods are planted around it.

The renowned trial attorney and secret serial killer now lives in his own private hell.

CHAPTER 72

Two weeks after Underwood's disappearance, a reporter asked security guard Dave Richards what he thought became of his old boss. Dave's reply was, "You're confusing me with somebody who gives a shit."

By late September 1988, the mystery of the missing celebrity lawyer was finally pushed off the front pages of Florida newspapers. NASA's resumption of space shuttle flights was now the big story. Especially, after the Challenger disaster that took the lives of seven astronauts.

No one ever regarded Underwood's loss as a disaster. Most people who had dealings with him, including other attorneys, said "good riddance". Many more, including Cassie, Tony, Malcolm Crothers and of course, Richards and PJ, were overjoyed.

Russell Underwood had vanished forever from a world that was so much better off without him.

PJ now looks once again at a crinkled piece of paper out of the past. The one that contained the two line poem written at age fourteen...

"The rest of us stand in a circle and suppose,
While the riddle sits in the middle and knows."

Whatever happened to Underwood is the new riddle. It will be kept in the middle.

At least until PJ finishes something else he has started to write.

EPILOGUE

In 1991, Florida courts made several important decisions regarding Preston's will and Underwood's demise. The relentless pursuit of justice by PJ had finally paid off. Cassie became the rightful heir to what remained of the Jennings fortune. But she took only enough money to cover her legal expenses. She put what was left into charitable trusts. And she did one more thing.

Preston Dylan Jennings once told her, "It's nice to be important, but it's more important to be nice." So she did something she knew he'd think was nice. His beloved Presthaven was awarded to a fellow Welshman, Malcolm Crothers. It is now a much needed assisted living facility for people like her dear old Luke.

By 1992, Tony Roselli and Manny Delgado had established a Florida franchise of upscale, award-winning DolceAmore restaurants. Manny got out of the cabaret business and moved to Key West where he and wife Renee manage one of the larger eateries.

In 1995, ten years after he lost an ear in the Everglades, Detective Sergeant Michael Gibson was very definitely retired. But there were still times when old Gibby hankered for a little law and order action. That's why wife Adrienne had carefully hidden away the old Smith & Wesson.

As for the million dollars that arrived so mysteriously decades ago, Cassie transferred it to her son's account. But it came from a biological father PJ wanted no part of, even in death. So it was donated to The Battered Women and Children Foundation.

Maybe he should have kept some of that money. He's quit the legal profession to become a struggling, still unpublished author. But hopes to change his luck soon. It's now 2010, and he's just finished writing a book based on his mom's life.

He's calling it "A Million To One."

This is a transplanted New Yorker's first novel. Ed deMartin was born in Manhattan, raised in Queens, graduated college from Brooklyn and spent plenty of family time in The Bronx. Father of four. Grandfather of seven. He is now retired in Naples, Florida where he met his wife, Marie.

He's an award-winning designer and writer/ director of films. Formerly a principal in the communications and design firm of DMCD (*deMartin, Marona, Cranstoun & Downes*). DMCD created corporate and entertainment films, identification programs and numerous visitor experiences for museums as well as several world expos and three presidential libraries. (For Lyndon B. Johnson, Richard M. Nixon and George H.W. Bush.)

Cover design by Michael and Ed deMartin.